PRIMAL MAN

PRIMAL MAN

R. J. CALSYN

iUniverse, Inc.
Bloomington

Primal Man

iUniverse books may be ordered through booksellers or by contacting:

iUniverse
1663 Liberty Drive
Bloomington, IN 47403
www.iuniverse.com
1-800-Authors (1-800-288-4677)

ISBN: 978-1-4620-4030-8 (sc)
ISBN: 978-1-4620-4031-5 (ebk)

Printed in the United States of America

iUniverse rev. date: 08/01/2011

DEDICATION

To my wife, Maria, friend and lover for over twenty-five years; our children (Soledad, Dylan, and Christopher) who give me more joy and pride than any one man deserves; and our grandchildren (Zoe, Margaret, Abigail, Ella, and Max) who constantly amaze me.

CONTENTS

PROLOGUE

Delphi, Missouri, does not appear in any road atlas. Nor can one find directions to the Temple of the Oracle through Mapquest. However, Delphi and all its inhabitants can be observed if the reader simply uses a little imagination. This mythical town is located south of St. Louis in lead mining country. Until recently Delphi was a quiet college town with very little crime. Now that has all changed.

Delphi was founded in the late nineteenth century by Greek pacifists who wanted to escape hostilities with their Turkish neighbors. Aristotle Heraclitis, who made his fortune as a bootlegger during Prohibition, established Delphi University in 1932. The mission of the campus is to develop well rounded leaders of society by integrating classical Greek culture with contemporary science and technology. The architecture of the campus is Greek revival. The two most distinctive features of the campus were not created by man. The Olympic Forest is an old growth forest that is home to thousands of species of fauna and flora. Scarlet oaks, shortleaf pines, cottonwoods, cypress, and cedar provide dense cover for red and grey fox, deer, wild turkeys, and thousands of rabbits and squirrels. The creeks and rivers that flow through the forest are home to leopard frogs, bass, carp, and perch. The Elysian Fields is a fifty-acre meadow of native prairie grasses, sunflowers, daylilies, honeysuckle, field mustard, chick weed, and thistle.

Over the past few years the Delphi Chamber of Commerce has sought to capitalize on Delphi's heritage by developing its own Greek marketplace, the Agora. The Hedonist Bakery sells fresh pita bread, baklava, and other pastries. Olives, figs, feta cheese, olive oil, roditis, retsina, ouzo, and other delicacies can be obtained at Dionysius Grocery. The Parthenon Restaurant serves outstanding gyro sandwiches and the best mousaka in the state. At Homer's Imports one can buy a plethora of Greek trinkets: replicas of the Parthenon, statues of the gods, pottery with classical motifs, carpets with geometric designs, religious icons, and dolls dressed in costumes from the time of Sophocles through the Ottoman domination.

The most recent enterprise to open its doors on the Agora is the Delphi Oracle. To promote the Oracle's business, young children dressed in Greek tunics, garlands, and sandals circulate through the Agora with flyers describing the services of the Oracle and location of the temple. The temple entrance is framed by two gigantic Doric columns that are out of proportion compared to the rest of the structure. Petitioners first enter a small ante room where they are greeted by an attractive priestess dressed in a white peplos fastened with a silver brooch. Her long ebony hair is pulled back and held in place with decorative combs. Reverently, she explains the sacred customs for interacting with the Oracle. Only one patron may enter the inner sanctum at a time and only one question is permitted. The sanctuary itself is a fifteen foot square. The walls are adorned with murals depicting famous scenes of Greek mythology. The perimeter of the sanctuary's floor is punctured with small iron grates from which mysterious vapors rise. The aroma varies depending on the mood of the Oracle herself. Sometimes the bouquet is jasmine, lavender, or other pleasing floral scents. The Oracle burns incense when she is in a more religious or ceremonial mood. If she is angry or gloomy, the smell of rotten eggs or other foul odor rises from the ground and nearly suffocates the client. The Oracle resides below the terrazzo floor and is not visible to the petitioner. After she makes her prophecy, the priestess appears from the mysterious mist to escort the supplicant from the temple. The offering for the divination is $25.

Most citizens of Delphi have welcomed the Oracle to the Agora. They believe that she is harmless and good for business. However, some traditionalists are outraged by the lack of authenticity. They complain that the Oracle operates more like a gypsy fortune teller than Phythia. They are particularly upset that small Roma looking children are being used as hucksters to stir up business. The dissenters also object to the "aroma therapy" being practiced by this impostor. They argue that it is ludicrous to imply that the vapors that rose from the Oracle's chamber varied according to her mood. The gas that rose from the temple floor of the original Oracle was not man made; rather, mother earth released the gas into the temple's bowels. Those vapors induced an altered state of consciousness and garbled speech in Phythia which necessitated that her prophecies be interpreted by a temple priest.

The city fathers listened patiently to the complaints of the traditionalists as well as the endorsements of the prophet's supporters. In their report they concluded that the new Oracle was providing a worthwhile service, complying with all local ordinances, and paying taxes. They reminded the traditionalists that the leaders of ancient Greece allowed the original Oracle to continue practicing her trade even though her methods had been questioned by some citizens. The community leaders ended their public hearing by encouraging the traditionalists and all residents of Delphi to practice the Greek virtue of tolerance in their interactions with the Oracle and every other citizen of their idyllic community.

BOOK ONE

PRIMAL MAN STIRS THE CAULDRON

The life of theoretical philosophy is the best and happiest a man can lead. Few men are capable of it (and then only intermittently). For the rest there is a second-best way of life, that of moral virtue and practical wisdom. (Aristotle) Philosophy is to the real world as masturbation is to sex. (Karl Marx)

CHAPTER 1:
GRAHAM HUNTER SEPTEMBER 23

Detective Graham Hunter sat alone in his office reading the file of Primal Man, the campus flasher at Delphi University. He was not enthusiastic about being assigned to this case, but he was resigned. The only way to receive a more important and interesting assignment was to expose the offender. There had been two incidents. Both times Primal Man wore nothing but a ski mask, gloves, and a black vinyl raincoat. To ensure that his victims took notice of his manliness he adorned his erect penis with a neon orange condom. He had not touched or spoken with either of his victims. Meekly, he had simply dropped an index card signed "Primal Man" at the feet of his prey. The messages contained both a maxim and a warning. The first card read: "Men are hunters; women are gatherers; gather yourself home." The second card declared: "A woman needs a man to protect her; don't leave home without one."

Hunter did not believe that Primal Man was dangerous. Not only were his messages fairly tame, but the victims described his demeanor as anxious and timid. His encounters were brief, allowing just enough time to flash the orange spear and leave his calling card before scampering into the forest. Unlike many exhibitionists he was not a risk taker. He did not expose himself in populated places; nor did he linger and talk with his prey. The flasher only confronted his quarry in dark, isolated locations. Even though he had caused considerable emotional upset in his victims, Hunter doubted that Primal Man was capable of physical violence. Nevertheless, he wanted to catch the perpetrator soon. Not only was Hunter concerned about the women of Delphi University, but he knew that his fellow cops would continue to shower him with sarcasm until the case was solved. A package of orange condoms had already appeared on his desk with a simple note, "To a fellow dick."

Hunter left the precinct building at 8 pm ready for a good night's sleep. However, Maria Flores, the local crime reporter for the *Delphi Scribe*, had other ideas.

"Detective Hunter, can I buy you a drink?"

"Ms. Flores, are you asking me out on a date?"

"Don't flatter yourself, Hunter. This is strictly business. I want to ask you about the campus flasher. My sources tell me you have been assigned the case."

"Maria, you know as much as I do. I haven't interviewed anyone yet, and there is nothing in the files that hasn't been released to the public."

The detective wasn't being totally honest. The information about the orange condom had not been shared with the public, so that the police could distinguish any future actions by Primal Man from those of copycats.

"Hunter, you're lying, but I won't pursue you tonight. I am too tired. I already have enough information for the lead article in tomorrow's paper. We'll continue this dance another time. Good night."

Too bad, thought Graham. He wouldn't mind dirty dancing with Maria Flores. She was a bright, attractive woman whose reporting was fair and honest. He didn't know much about her personal life except that she was a native of Chile. He didn't think she was married (no ring), but was there a boyfriend? The thought of tangoing with Maria Flores in the future provided Graham with a whole new perspective regarding the case of Primal Man.

Hunter defied the cultural stereotype of the hard-boiled, beer drinking, hot tempered detective. He abhorred violence of all kinds. He had been a conscientious objector during the Vietnam War and had performed his alternative service at a state mental hospital. Although he knew all of the arguments of the just war theorists, he was not convinced. He had read too much history; he knew that millions had died needlessly in countless "just wars." He also was a great admirer of Mahatma Gandhi and Martin Luther King. With their discipline, patience, and inspiration, they had proven that great political change could be accomplished with a strategy of non-violence and civil disobedience. His own commitment to pacifism sometimes caused him conflicts in his profession, but he took pride in never having discharged his weapon in over twenty years of police work. Injustices of any kind made him boiling mad, but over the years he had learned to control his emotions. His need to stifle any expression of anger was the result of an emotional scare at a farewell party for a classmate during his junior year in high school. A drunken basketball player hit him for no reason and opened a big gash over his right eye. He reacted instinctively, tackling the drunk and pounding his head on the cement driveway. It took three friends to pull him off his victim. His uncontrolled violent reaction frightened him so much that he swore he would never raise his fists in anger again. For the most part he had kept that pledge, but sometimes he struggled to keep his rage under control. The cruelty that he observed in his work stirred his insides. His colleagues, however, rarely saw his emotions. Behind his back they called Hunter "the cold one." Of course he could have been bestowed that nickname, because he was also known to like his beer.

Like his hero, Colin Dexter's Inspector Morse, Graham was prone to brooding, depression, and insomnia. His tastes in music were more eclectic than those of Morse. In addition to classical music he listened to folk, country, and blues. He also studied philosophy. At night when sleep would not come, he fantasized about how one of the great masters would tackle the practical problems of crime investigation that he faced every day. He found himself more aligned with Hume and the empiricists than with the rationalists like Descartes. It seemed incredibly foolish and arrogant to have more faith in your mind than your senses. Prejudices and prior experience colored the thought processes of most humans.

The biographies of the philosophers also fascinated Graham. Many times he imagined one of the masters conducting a crime investigation using their own unique method of inquiry. Aristotle and Kant would operate more like Hercule Poirot—very direct, analytical, logical, but with little emotion. Socrates, on the other hand, would behave more like Columbo, using a more indirect method of interrogation with each question leading to a more nuanced discussion of the evidence with his witness. He would make the interviewee feel like he was a partner in the search for truth. He would also approach his task with passion and wonder; each discovery would lead him to exclaim "Eureka." Graham wished that he had the enthusiasm and intuition of the man who drank the hemlock. Unfortunately, he saw himself as a boring, predictable, plodding empiricist who would finally discover the truth, but with much less flair than Socrates.

Still preoccupied with thoughts about Primal Man and Maria Flores, Hunter put on Bach's Fifth Brandenburg Concerto. He could never articulate why he liked the chamber music of Bach so much. His themes were expressive but restrained by mathematical rules. Although Bach did not stir his emotions as much as Mahler, the music was more comforting. Sleep finally came as the concerto reached the finale.

CHAPTER 2:
HILDA GERMAN SEPTEMBER 24

Dr. Hilda German stared vacantly at her notes as she prepared to take command of the Women's Studies Program at Delphi University. She had been extremely nervous the night before, fussing with the agenda and re-writing her opening remarks. Now she had difficulty focusing on her speech and the larger task before her; flashbacks of the events that had propelled her into her new position kept entering her mind. German had always doubted the commitment to feminism of the prior director, Shelia Benson. Shelia was soft; she was a compromiser. There was no angry edge to her. Moreover, she was married to the Dean of Arts and Letters. Hilda didn't believe any women could call herself a true feminist and be sleeping with a man, particularly one who held a more powerful position than she did. Two issues had compelled her to challenge Benson for leadership of the Women's Studies Program.

First, Benson had failed to support the Lesbian Student Association in their campaign to prohibit the Sigma PI fraternity from holding the "Sexy Legs" competition. Benson, the traitor, refused to endorse Hilda's resolution calling on the campus administration to cancel this sexist contest. She had argued that "freedom of speech" and "freedom of assembly" were important principles at a university that trumped everything else. In her view all university organizations, regardless of how abhorrent their ideology, must be granted these rights. Benson reminded the students and faculty that the event was co-sponsored by the Delta Chi sorority and that both men and women were free to enter the competition. She suggested that the Lesbian Student Association organize an educational protest rather than attempt to prohibit the Greeks from having their contest. German had given an impassioned rebuttal, begging her colleagues not to abandon their younger sisters and to take a stand against the sexism that was rampant on campus. She had argued that the women of Delta Chi or any woman who entered the "Sexy Legs" event were innocent dupes of a male dominated society. Her resolution had lost by one vote.

Benson's refusal to help scuttle the new Program in Male Studies (PMS) in the Faculty Senate had pushed Hilda over the edge. As chair of the campus curriculum committee Benson could have used procedural tactics to prevent a full Faculty Senate vote on establishing the new program which was rooted in the sexist ideology of sociobiology and evolutionary psychology. When Hilda had asked Benson why she hadn't used her discretionary power to quash the PMS, she had calmly replied that it was an issue of "academic freedom." "You academic whore," German had screamed at Benson. It was the first time in thirty-five years at Delphi University that she had lost her cool and showed her raw emotions

Now she was prepared to right the ship and return the Women's Studies Program to its radical roots. The days of accommodation with male reactionaries were over. Benson and the other young women professors hadn't been part of the feminist revolution at Delphi University. They didn't know what the more senior women had endured in terms of lower salaries, smaller offices, less financial support for their research, and general contempt from their male colleagues. German was convinced that all of the gains for which the older women had fought would be lost if the program did not take a forceful stand every time the sexist elements on campus reared their ugly heads.

A knock on her door abruptly ended her reflections. Sara Chaste, her long-time friend, had come to offer her support as she began her reign as the new Director of the Women's Studies Program. Hilda collected her notes as Sara reached up to adjust Hilda's tie and button her suit jacket. The suit and tie were a gift from Sara who had chided her friend, "If you are going to dress like a man, then dress like an executive. You are a leader now." German was 6'1" and toothpick thin. Recently she had been using a cane because of a bad knee. She had snow white wavy hair that was cut short and parted on the left side. She wore no make-up or jewelry. German preferred men's clothes; she felt that they were more comfortable. Sara took her friend's arm and together they made the journey across the courtyard to the Susan B. Anthony Conference Room.

German tapped her cane lightly to get the attention of her colleagues who were engaged in various conversations in the conference room. She was determined that meetings of the group would start on time and follow parliamentary procedure now that she was director. Meetings that started late and meandered from topic to topic were a symptom of how casual and undisciplined the entire program had become during Shelia Benson's tenure. Irritated with the continued loquaciousness of her colleagues Hilda angrily rapped her cane on the base of the metal lectern. Silence immediately filled the room; in unison twenty women turned their heads and gave German their undivided attention. She cleared her throat, peered over her reading glasses at her audience, and began her address.

"My dear sisters, thank you for giving me this opportunity to serve you and all of the women of Delphi University. As you know I am deeply concerned that the Women's Studies Program has lost the revolutionary vision that guided its birth some twenty-five years ago. This organization has become complacent, too willing to let our enemies hide behind the banners of free speech and academic freedom while they promulgate their misogynist ideology and engage in their sexist rituals. I implore you to join me in vigorously challenging sexism at Delphi University in every venue (classrooms, dorms, athletic fields, academic departments, faculty governance, and even the boardroom). I know that some of you, especially my younger colleagues, feel that the revolution has been won and that sexism is on the decline. You believe that most of our male colleagues are now with us and that we should change our tactics from direct action to education and negotiation. Two years ago I would have agreed with you. Through the efforts of this group of feminists significant progress had been achieved, but where are we today? Last year more sexual harassment complaints were filed than ever before. Even though our current President is a woman, five female faculty members were denied tenure. The evidence is clear. Unless we renew our activism, my fellow sisters, women will remain second class citizens in the university. Throughout the year I will ask you to serve on various committees to gather evidence of sexism, secure signatures on various petitions, and do whatever else it takes to protect the interests of the women in our community. Together we can make the feminist dream a reality at Delphi University. Thank you."

The audience responded with fierce clapping and raised fists. The remainder of the meeting was taken up with the organization of various ad hoc task forces to deal with specific issues. There was a task force to oppose the "Sexy Legs" contest. A group was organized to investigate what was being taught in the PMS curriculum. Another committee was created to assist the women who had been denied tenure in preparing their appeals. A final task force was established to investigate the sexual harassment cases.

CHAPTER 3:
MARGO ELLY SEPTEMBER 24

Quietly Dr. Margo Elly, Professor of Biochemistry, left the meeting of the Women's Studies Program. She had no time for the small talk that took place during the social hour that followed the formal meeting. During German's speech she had sat alone in the back row. She appeared taller than 5'6", because she was sitting rigidly upright on the orthopedic cushion that had become her constant companion since her car accident five years ago. Her wrinkled face appeared locked in a perpetual grimace. Chronic back pain was one explanation for her constant frown, but contempt for her colleagues was a strong rival hypothesis.

Elly did not volunteer to work on any of the committees. She thought most of the women in the program were losers. They were a gaggle of complainers who spouted slogans, but who knew nothing about logic and strategic planning. Other than her gonads she had little in common with the other women in the room. Margo's identity was not as a feminist but as a hard scientist. Despite her disdain for her colleagues Margo never missed a meeting of the Women's Studies Program. Her attendance at these gatherings had become a masochistic ritual that she endured because of a dogged belief that her presence ultimately benefited her students. Periodically her sacrifice was rewarded, when one of her graduate students received a scholarship from the program.

After a ten-minute walk Elly arrived at the Euclidean Science Building and stealthily slipped into her office and closed the door. She had intended to work on a manuscript, but she couldn't concentrate. She felt physically sick. Recently her brain had been overtaken by a disgusting image of George Savage, Director of PMS, lying naked in bed with Emily Smith. Emily was the only undergraduate ever permitted to work in Elly's lab. It had been a productive relationship (four journal articles and two small grants). With Margo's help her protégée had been awarded a graduate fellowship in biochemistry at Harvard.

Then George Savage entered the picture. Emily had attended his lecture "The Territorial Imperative Lives." She was immediately captivated by the man and the topic. She had never been exposed to the evolutionary psychology theory that he espoused or any other course on human origins. Elly had tried desperately to discourage her student from becoming involved with Savage. She told her that his ideas were not based on science and that he had a reputation as a lecher, but Emily would not listen. Within three weeks he had seduced her. Not only was he sleeping with her, but he had convinced her to reject the fellowship at Harvard. He persuaded her that she needed to explore her new interest in sociobiology and evolutionary psychology before committing to a career in biochemistry. Emily agreed and moved in with Savage. She was eager to study and experience the origins and movements of primitive men, both dead and alive.

Margo Elly was mystified by Savage's ability to charm Emily and countless other co-eds. He was not a handsome man. Broken capillaries in his bulbous nose and a massive beer gut indicated a life of heavy drinking. Nevertheless, many young women described his countenance as rugged and mysterious. They also loved his long, untamed straw colored hair. His aqua eyes were described as devilish and fun loving. Savage's wardrobe added to his mystic. Like his hero, Willie Nelson, he wore a red bandana and a love bead necklace. His blue jeans were held in place by a belt adorned with a large silver and turquoise buckle. Cowboy boots made from the skins of rattlesnakes completed the ensemble. Savage's carefully crafted physical persona was not the only reason for his success with young women. He also knew how to tell a story. His description of how man's vegetarian ancestors climbed down from the trees and became blood thirsty killers captivated even his sharpest critics. Even more entertaining were Savage's tales about his own origins. The man claimed that his maternal grandmother had been the daughter of the famous Apache warrior, Geronimo, and that her husband had been the son of General George Custer.

Margo Elly's vision of George Savage was much different than that of her younger sisters. She hated everything about the man. Disgusting images of him rubbing Emily's thighs with his dirty, rough, stubby fingers kept flashing before her. She had fantasies of chopping off his prick with her meat clever, but how would she find such a tiny piece of flesh hidden beneath the rolls of fat that hung over his belt. Her mind kept jumping from graphic pictures of Savage violating Emily to sadistic scenes in which she murdered the pig in the vilest manner imaginable. Eventually she regained control of her thought processes sufficiently to hatch a plan to rid Emily and Delphi University of George Savage.

CHAPTER 4:
PRIMAL MAN SEPTEMBER 25

Primal Man sat alone in his dorm room reading the *Delphi Scribe's* account of his most recent expedition to enlighten the co-eds of Delphi University. He had made the front page. Now everyone would take him seriously. He had been hurt and angry when the press had hidden the news of his first mission on page 32.

Professor Savage was right. Biology dictated that the physically stronger male should be the hunter and protector. Women were programmed to produce and take care of the children. The feminists had upset the balance of nature by demanding that women be allowed to compete with men in the workplace. Birth control had made things even worse. Not only could women now delay child bearing, but they could remain childless for life. How was the species going to survive if the majority of women took that position? Birth control had also made whores of modern women. Too often they had the audacity to initiate sex, rather than waiting for the male to be the aggressor. Worse yet, many modern women had more than one partner. Although nature demanded that men plant their seed in multiple wombs to freshen the gene pool, women were suppose to be monogamous and submissive to a life-long mate.

Growing up had been difficult for Primal Man. Everyone made fun of his stutter. Not even his teachers displayed any empathy for his malady. They ignored his pleas to substitute written work for oral assignments. The boys tortured him by mimicking his speech. However, the pain inflicted by teenage girls was the worst humiliation. Most of the time they were oblivious to his presence, or they took evasive action when he approached. On the rare occasions that he had summoned the courage to ask one of these sluts to dance with him or go on a date, they refused. They preferred to be wall flowers rather than be seen as his partner.

College broads were even more merciless in their interactions with him. They paraded in front of him almost naked. Mid-drift blouses shamelessly exposed their boobs and navels. Tight fitting jeans accented their asses. However, if he dared to speak to these temptresses, they simply ignored him as they strutted toward their next victim. Now that he was Primal Man these bitches would take notice of him. He vowed to continue his crusade. Yes, he would spread the gospel of sociobiology and evolutionary psychology, even if it meant exposing himself and his message to every single co-ed on campus. They would listen or else.

CHAPTER 5:
GRAHAM HUNTER SEPTEMBER 25

Hunter was making little headway in his search for Primal Man. The victims had reported that the flasher was of average height and weight. They had no clue as to his race; the ski mask, gloves, and silence protected the exhibitionist's true identity. Although there had been several indecent exposure incidents in the past year, all of them had been "moonings." Most appeared to be fraternity pranks. A group of drunken adolescents would quickly drop their pants on the porch of a sorority house as some co-ed answered the doorbell; they then sprinted to a waiting car. No indecent exposure incidents involving a single offender had been reported prior to the appearance of Primal Man. A search of FBI files for other sex crimes had uncovered no other perpetrator with a similar modus operandi. A check of recent parolees from the state pen had also turned up no likely suspects. Hunter's instinct told him that Primal Man was not a habitual sex offender, but rather a young timid male college student who was having a difficult time competing for and with women. Of course that description applied to most of the male student population.

Hunter knew that he needed to solve the case quickly, or vigilantes would start harassing every male who was out after dark. Inflammatory editorials had already appeared in the campus and local newspaper. One railed about the incompetence of the police. Another warned parents to keep their daughters at home until someone eliminated the dangerous predator that was stalking the women of Delphi University. The county prosecutor was even more anxious than usual about public opinion. He was harassing Hunter on a daily basis to make an arrest. Unfortunately, he had no suspects.

Feeling frustrated Graham decided to call upon his old friend, Father Dominic Alongi, who was now the Catholic chaplain at Delphi

University. Graham had occasionally used Dom as a psychological profiler in helping him solve cases. Dom had a degree in counseling as well as theology, and he had been a prison chaplain for seven years before taking the job at Delphi University. Father Dominic was the one person with whom Graham could be totally honest, the one person to whom he could confess that Primal Man had him totally baffled.

Dom and Graham had been inseparable from kindergarten through high school. They made their first communions together, served as altar boys at hundreds of Masses, played on the same soccer team for ten years, and dated the same girls all through high school. Going to separate colleges had been a difficult decision for both of them. Hunter wanted to escape the Catholic ghetto as he called it and left for Indiana University on a soccer scholarship. Dominic could not pry himself from his Italian Catholic family. He chose St. Jude, the local Catholic college. It was during his freshmen year, away from Graham's influence, that Dominic had received his calling to the priesthood.

Hunter's college education had abruptly ended during his sophomore year when his father died in a construction accident. He returned home to help his mother raise his five younger siblings. Dom had been his salvation during that period. He played endless games of soccer, basketball, and jump rope with Graham's brothers and sisters when Graham no longer had the energy or patience. He ran errands for Graham's mother and prayed with her. Although Graham would do almost anything for his mother, he could no longer pray with her. His faith in God had dissolved slowly over the years. At first it had been intellectual disagreements with the Catholic Church over issues like papal infallibility and the Church's prohibition against birth control. With the untimely death of his father and the obvious suffering of his mother, his contempt for God and religion had become personal. Dom had known instinctively how to help him cope with his father's death. Depending on the situation the priest defused, channeled, or absorbed Graham's anger.

Graham and Dom remained close friends over the years. Dom had been a frequent dinner guest at the Hunter's home until Mrs. Hunter died of cancer six months ago. After Graham's siblings had sorted through her possessions and taken those items which had sentimental value, he was left alone with the remainder of her legacy. For weeks he had been unable to summon the energy to box-up his mother's clothes and personal items. Father Dominic had once again risen to the occasion to help his friend. Together they sorted and packed the remaining artifacts for Catholic Charities. During that time Dom helped Graham reminisce and grieve for both of his parents.

Today the priest greeted the detective with a huge bear hug and escorted his friend into the parlor. "Now Detective Hunter, how can this humble servant of the church help a dedicated protector of the people."

With a mock bow Graham responded in kind, "Father, Satan is in our midst. I have come to ask your help in apprehending Primal Man. Then you can exorcise the devil that makes him flash his weenie at co-eds, and I can get back to catching real criminals."

"So Primal Man has you stumped. I doubt that our young friend is dangerous; he is just confused, particularly about sex. There is a lot more titillation going on today than when we were young. Primal Man sees a lot of female flesh, but it is unavailable to him. Frustrated he resorts to exposing himself."

"Dom, that's great pop psychology, but I think your description probably fits half of the male students at Delphi University. Any suggestions for limiting the list of suspects?"

"Only one. Primal Man may be a disciple of the campus chauvinist, George Savage."

"Fill me in. I'm not following."

"Savage is an anthropologist at Delphi University who espouses the perspective of evolutionary psychology and sociobiology, the reactionaries who believe that occupational roles are predestined by gender. 'Primal Man' is the generic name that Savage uses to represent the traditional hunting and family protection roles that men assumed when they first walked the earth. He has developed the Program in Male Studies that offers courses which promulgate this sexist garbage. I am afraid that some young men at Delphi, confused and intimidated by the changing sex roles in our society, are swallowing this crap. Quite understandably the women faculty and students, particularly those in the Women's Studies Program, are outraged. They have written several op-ed pieces in the campus newspaper condemning Savage and his views."

"Where can I find Savage?"

"His office is in the Murky Social Sciences Building, but I doubt that he will be very cooperative. You would probably learn more by mingling with the male students who support him."

"Dom, at forty-four I think that I am too old and gray to blend in with undergraduates and not be noticed."

"How about that young detective, O'Rourke? Isn't he a student here?"

"Yeah, that might work. O'Rourke's a good kid. I'll ask the chief to loan him to me for a few weeks. Thanks, Dom. I owe you a dinner."

When he arrived home Graham poured himself a glass of Rioja to unwind and put on his Tom Rush CD. When Rush sang "Good-by Momma," the first words of *"Child's Song,"* his thoughts shifted from Primal Man to his parents. Seeing Dom always triggered those memories. Hunter had never moved out of his parents' huge four bedroom house. He had pleaded with his mother to sell the house after all of his siblings had moved out, but she couldn't part with it. Mrs. Hunter had grown old and comfortable with the house and her neighborhood. Every day she walked two blocks to St. Gabriel's for morning mass and stopped at Alongi's bakery for fresh bread and a pastry for Graham. She had loved to sit on her porch swing and watch the children skip rope and play other games on the sidewalk. Many times Graham had tried to sell his mother on the idea of a two family flat; she could have the first floor and he would take the second. He wanted his own place where he could have some privacy and entertain friends, perhaps even a girlfriend. His mother dismissed the idea without discussion. She had emotionally blackmailed him, leaving him sulking and frustrated every time the topic was broached.

Now it was Graham's turn to drag his feet. He knew it made good economical and emotional sense to sell the house and find something smaller now that his mother was gone. His siblings had offered to help paint and fix-up the place, but he couldn't summon the energy necessary to move on. Tonight he just stared at the wedding picture of his parents; slowly, the tears began to roll down his cheeks. Images of his parents flooded his mind. There was his dad, muscles bulging from both his shirt and his shorts, demonstrating how to properly kick a soccer ball when Graham was three. Then his mother appeared on the porch swing, gently gliding back and forth with her coal black hair blowing in the wind as she peeled apples for a pie. He smiled at the memory of his father patting his mother on the fanny and "copping a feel." He saw his mother massaging his dad's back after a long day at work and kissing his neck in between strokes. Then the sad memories seized his mind—the image of his father's casket and his mother's vacant stare at the wake. Finally, there was his mother's casket and Graham's own empty gaze.

Rumination about his parents always led Graham to yet another internal debate about the existence and character of God. Catholicism had been a central part of his life for many years. Although he had logically rejected its doctrines, he would never be free of them. Until he reached puberty, Graham sincerely believed that he had a calling for the priesthood. His mother had encouraged his vocation. At the Catholic supply store they purchased holy cards with idealized images of the saints on the front and a brief biography on the back. They kept these treasures in a scrapbook which Graham still visited whenever he missed his mother. He marveled at the dedication and sacrifice of the men and women who served the poor. Francis of Assisi, John Bosco, and Father Damien of the lepers, were his favorites.

Hunter no longer considered the Catholic Church to be God's representative on Earth. How could a Church that sponsored the Inquisition be considered holy? Moreover, why didn't the Church use its considerable wealth to help the poor? Lately, Graham even questioned whether there was a God. Although he knew all of the arguments of Thomas Aquinas for the existence of God, he was not convinced. Only the theologian's argument that the beauty and order of the universe proved that there was a God had any meaning for him; the big bang explanation for the creation of the universe left him cold. However, Graham no longer believed in a God who took a personal interest in humans and periodically made interventions to assist them. He had seen too many prayers go unanswered. If God existed, he was an uncaring, disinterested, son-of-a-bitch. And Graham was angry as hell at him.

CHAPTER 6:
MARGO ELLY SEPTEMBER 27

Three days had passed since Margo Elly had formulated her plan to free Emily Smith from the clutches of George Savage. She had chosen to wait until late Friday evening to confront him, knowing that his office building would be virtually empty. Elly was so focused on her speech to Savage that she was oblivious to the scents that surrounded her as she crossed through the campus botanical gardens. Normally Margo's senses would be totally saturated by the beauty of the gardens. She had spent hours grading papers in this paradise, looking up frequently to enjoy the cornucopia of colors that enveloped her while she inhaled the fragrances of jasmine, lilac, and honey suckle. Today she only sensed hate.

It was twilight when she reached the Murky Social Sciences Building. The place appeared deserted. She knocked on Savage's door repeatedly, but there was no response. Finally, she simply pushed opened the door; the pig was sound asleep. His shirt and belt were loosened, exposing more hairy flesh than any sensitive human being should have to observe. Margo banged on the chauvinist's desk with her clenched fist. A startled Savage almost fell from his chair, but he quickly came to attention. Calmly he folded his arms across his enormous belly and surreptitiously fastened his belt. He was entombed behind a large desk with books and papers stacked high in precarious piles. On his left was a side table with a computer, scribbled notes, and a bottle of scotch. A side chair containing boxing gloves, sweaty gym shorts, and a jock strap stood guard on his right flank. At his back were bookshelves from floor to ceiling that were as disheveled as the man himself. Some books were laying flat; others were inverted with the binding facing the wall; interspersed were computer printouts and copies of journal articles. The materials were not arranged alphabetically, by topic, or by any other taxonomy. Elly was not surprised. George Savage had no discipline in his private life; why would anyone expect his professional life to be different? Margo felt her stomach tighten and her pulse quicken. The chaos in the office was suffocating her. She felt faint and wanted to flee, but her hatred of this pig provided her with enough energy and will power to temporarily ignore the weakness that pervaded her body. She drew back her shoulders and made herself as tall and menacing as possible.

Savage broke the silence, "And what brings the Ice Queen to the lair of the King of the Jungle?"

Elly was determined not to be provoked. "I am here on serious business, Savage. Either you convince Emily Smith to accept the fellowship at Harvard, or I will destroy you."

"And how do you propose to do that, my dear Margo?"

"Simple. I will convince as many of your prior conquests to file sexual harassment charges against you. We also have these color photos of how you treated your ex-wives. Take a look."

Savage's face turned scarlet with anger and anxiety as he examined the photos of his battered spouses, but he remained seated and tried to appear calm. "Sorry, sweetheart, it won't work. You have no case. All of the women who have had the pleasure of my bed were of legal age and fully consented, and I was never charged with spousal abuse. Who knows how those poor women were injured?"

"Don't be so cocky, dickhead! I have already spoken to several of your victims who are ready to press charges. Two feminist lawyers are willing to pursue their cases on a contingency basis. On the other hand, no one is going to defend your sorry ass for free! We don't need to win any of these cases to break you financially and make your life miserable for the next several years. Think about it, asshole! If Emily does not inform me that she has accepted the Harvard fellowship within three days, I will put my plan into action. By the way, having liquor in your office is against university policy." Margo turned on her heels, slammed the door, and sprinted down the hall. Savage stumbled clumsily from his chair and chased after her yelling obscenities, but he couldn't catch her.

Margo arrived at her home exhausted after her confrontation with Savage. Her heart was still pounding and she felt weak-kneed, but she had been cool under fire. She knew that she had frightened him. Margo was convinced that the sexist pig would cower and abandon his fling with Emily. She had no clue, however, regarding how her protégée would take Savage's rejection. Despite having worked closely with her for two years, Margo realized that she knew nothing of her student as a person. They had never talked about anything but work. She had no knowledge of Emily's family or friends, or even simple things like her taste in music or her favorite cuisine. What would happen when the chauvinist kicked her out of his bed? Would she go ballistic and trash the lab, or would she become distraught and try to kill herself? Margo tried to comfort herself with the memory of how logically Emily had attacked every problem that they had faced together in the lab. Emily would get over George Savage; she would see him for the self-absorbed slob that he was; she would take the Harvard fellowship. Or would she? Anxiety and doubt seized Margo's entire being.

More than ever Margo needed the comfort of her nightly bath. Meticulously she prepared everything required for this sacred ritual. She plugged in the CD player and put on the sitar music of Ravi Shankar. Slowly she removed her clothes, carefully folding every piece before placing them in the hamper. Her earrings and necklace were returned to their assigned spot in her jewelry box. She sat down at her dressing table and brushed her hair one hundred strokes like she had done every day since her twelfth birthday. Then she turned on the water, fussed with the temperature until it was perfect, and added her favorite foaming bath oil to the water. She arranged three candles around the room to create an even more sensual atmosphere. Four bath sponges were close at hand for her cleansing ritual. First, she used the abrasive pumice to remove the calluses from her feet. Then she scraped her skin with the sisal back scrubber, removing the dry dead skin from her body and releasing the toxins trapped in the fat cells beneath the skin. Finally, she used the soft loofa and fina sponges for a gentle exfoliation. Slowly she lowered herself into the rose scented foam until the bubbles reached her chin. No one could touch her here—not George Savage, not anyone.

CHAPTER 7:
EMILY SMITH, SEPTEMBER 27

Emily Smith paced back and forth across the living room of George Savage's apartment. It was 9 pm and George still was not home. She called his office, but there was no answer. She was terrified to ride her bicycle across campus at the late hour, fearing an attack by Primal Man. Despite her fear of the flasher and the other creatures of the night, she was determined to save her man. Recently he had begun drinking heavily and was prone to violent mood swings. The charming figure who had mesmerized her two months ago had become an unpredictable emotional mess. At one moment he would be totally overtaken by his anger, slamming doors, throwing books, and cursing everyone including himself. In an instant he would change into a scared little boy, crying uncontrollably. She was frightened by his emotional lability, but she convinced herself that it was temporary. The pressure from Hilda German and her feminist allies had pushed him over the edge. Emily persuaded herself that Savage would become his jovial self again if she stuck by him. She just had to be more understanding and loving.

Emily placed the necklace with her whistle and mace spray around her neck and mounted her bike. There was a full moon. The additional light should make it safer she thought, but then she remembered the horrible crimes attributed to the power of the full moon. She pedaled as fast as she could. The silence was eerie, and she could feel her heart racing. She heard the rustling of leaves; suddenly something darted in front of her. She slammed on her brakes and nearly toppled head first over the handlebars to avoid hitting a possum searching for a midnight snack. She took a deep breath and resumed her journey. She could not stop obsessing about Primal Man, however. What would she do if the pervert emerged from the forest? She clutched her mace canister and said a silent prayer.

Although Savage's apartment was only a ten minute bike ride to campus, Emily felt the journey would never end. She wanted to get out of the darkness and into the light. Finally, she reached the social science building and dismounted. A loud crashing sound startled her. She dropped her bike and grabbed for her whistle. A raccoon was calmly pawing through the contents of a toppled trashcan. She heaved a sigh of relief, picked up her bike, and walked to the entrance of the building. The doors were locked. Now what! She decided to walk to the rear of the building where Savage's office was. The campus was not well lighted except for the entrances to the buildings. She could barely see where she was walking; the moonlight could not pierce the dense tree line that surrounded the building. Every twig that she stepped on, and every puddle that she sloshed through, made her clutch her mace. Finally, she reached the rear of the building; the light was still on in George's office. Quickly she retraced her steps and noticed a campus police car parked under a tree on the side of the building. The cop was asleep. Emily rapped on the window and the officer jumped to attention. Slowly he slid out of the car and wiped the sleep from his eyes. Irritably he grunted "What's the problem, little lady?"

"Professor Savage still isn't home, and it is very late. I called him at his office but there was no answer."

"And what is your relationship to Professor Savage?"

"Uh, Uh, I am his niece," stuttered Emily. "I'm visiting him for awhile."

"What makes you think he is on campus and not out partying somewhere?"

"The light in his office is still on. Please, can't we just take a look? I'm afraid he might have had a heart attack or something."

"Okay, let's go."

After trying a multitude of keys the officer finally found the right one to access the building. It took the rotund policeman forever to climb the three floors to Savage's office. Emily's impatience escalated with every passing minute. Nevertheless, she realized that she was totally dependent on the big oaf, so she stifled her rage. Finally, they reached the office. They pounded on the door, but there was no response. They tried to open the door, but it was locked. Again the policeman fumbled with his keys for what seemed an eternity before he found the right one. Savage was slumped forward with his head lying on the desk. Occasionally his body would twitch violently, and his breathing was labored and loud.

"Looks like your uncle may be a bit hung over, miss. What do you want to do now?"

"Could you take us home? We only live a few minutes from campus."

After radioing the dispatcher and filling her in on the details, including the professor's state of intoxication, the policeman pushed the inebriated anthropologist back in his chair and secured him with handcuffs. Carelessly he pushed the chair down the corridor to the elevator. Emily ran along side, trying to make sure that her man did not fall out of the makeshift wheelchair. Then Emily and the policeman squeezed Savage into the back seat of the patrol car and drove to his apartment.

The sun was setting before George Savage awoke from his drunken stupor. Emily brought him coffee in bed, but he yelled at her to go away. An hour later he slowly rose from his bed and made his way to the bathroom where he sought relief from his hangover. Quickly he swallowed a mixture of aspirin, Malox, and toothpaste.

Once again Emily offered him coffee, but he refused. Instead he prepared a meal of dry toast with a milk chaser. He then grabbed a beer from the fridge and went to his study to work on a manuscript, but Emily had other ideas. She needed some answers. She told Savage that his violent mood swings had to end, or she was going to move out.

He laughed at her. "Emily, I am old enough to be your father. You're in no position to give me orders. I'm getting sick of you behaving like a nagging wife. You need to talk less and fuck more."

Hurt and humiliated Emily retreated to the spare bedroom and shut the door. A few minutes later she heard Savage slam the front door. She suspected that he was going to the liquor store for more tonic to help him escape his demons. After crying for an hour Emily packed her suitcase and headed for the bus station. She needed the sanctuary of her home. Neither Elly nor Savage cared a damn about her. To Elly she was just a worker bee. To Savage she was just another sexual conquest.

CHAPTER 8:
GRAHAM HUNTER SEPTEMBER 30

Hunter was having an afternoon snack of Cheetos and Coke when Kevin O'Rourke entered his office. O'Rourke's freckles and uncontrollable red hair made him look much younger than his twenty-seven years.

"Kevin, good to see you again. Have you had a chance to read the file?"

"Yes, sir."

"Kevin, if we are going to work together, you will have to drop 'sir' from your vocabulary and call me 'Graham' or 'Hunter.' 'Sir' makes me feel old. So, what do you think about the case?"

"Primal Man is obviously a pervert."

"Anything else?"

"He also appears scared to death of women, but aren't we all?"

"Do you know anything about the Program in Male Studies at Delphi?"

"Not much other than the feminists hate it."

"How about an anthropology professor named Savage?"

"He has a reputation as an entertaining lecturer, but he's a lech. He tries to screw every attractive woman who takes his classes. He hit upon Officer O'Malley last year, but she got him good. She kept stringing him along until after the grades were turned in. Then she agreed to meet him for a drink. As he greeted her in the parking lot of the bar the scumbag put his arm around her waist just as she predicted. Immediately she whacked him in the balls, put him in a choke hold, and told him he was under arrest for assault. After he pleaded like a baby, she let him go with a warning to leave his female students alone, or she and her fellow officers would castrate him."

"Good for O'Malley. I want you to talk to her and find out all you can about Savage. Then make an appointment with Father Alongi, the

Catholic chaplain at Delphi University. He is an old friend of mine. He thinks Primal Man might be a student in the PMS. Enroll in one of Savage's courses; the department will pay the tuition. One last thing, this is an undercover assignment, so lose your tie and your gun."

"Come on, Graham, do I seem that naive?"

"No comment. Give me an update in two days."

Maria Flores was again waiting for Hunter as he left the precinct at 6:30 pm. Hunter was startled by the spontaneous bulge that filled his pants. He deftly shifted his briefcase to shield his excitement.

"Hunter, I am increasing the size of my bribe. Let me buy you dinner tonight. What type of cuisine makes you the most loquacious?"

"Maria, are you talking dirty to me?"

"I think we should stop this banter and get something to eat. How about the Parthenon? I am in the mood for Greek."

"Perfect. The mousaka and roditis will help me forget Primal Man."

"Wrong answer. We want a diet that restores your memory and loosens your tongue."

"Sorry, just prolonging the joust. Let's go. I'm starved."

With great difficulty Hunter had gotten his excitement under control by thinking of a big bowl of beets. Beets were the only food that made him gag. He had first used this visualization to deflate his penis in sixth grade. Staring at Nancy Furillo's massive tits had created a throbbing boner that lasted for nearly an hour. Nothing had worked to alleviate his discomfort. Neither praying to the Virgin, nor imagining Sister Peraclita naked, had weakened his hard, but the thought of eating beets had shrunk it instantly. Now Hunter wondered if he would ever be able to look directly at Maria Flores without getting an erection, or seeing beets sprout from her ebony locks.

During the two-block walk to the Parthenon Graham tried to regain control. There were no further eruptions from his penis, but he was distracted. He had always preferred brunettes to blondes, even among movie stars. Sophia Loren was a heavenly goddess; Marilyn Monroe was just a painted doll. The 5'6" Maria Flores was almost as curvy as Sophia, and her lips were as full and as inviting as the movie star's. Her big brown eyes were not only sexy but full of life. Graham's uncontrolled attraction to Maria Flores scared him; he had always thought he was more in command of his emotions. The thought of making love to her was indeed exciting. However, he was not sure that he wanted to be "in love," because that would mean losing control of his feelings and being at the mercy of the Chilean journalist. He hadn't let any woman get close to him in eons. Looking at the menu and ordering had allowed Hunter to pretend for the moment that this dinner was just a business meeting, but he had great difficulty maintaining that illusion while they waited for their food.

"Hunter, you seem distracted? I wouldn't think a campus flasher would have such an impact on a tough guy like you. There must be something more sinister about this case. You're too experienced, Graham. Come clean."

"There have been two victims. The flasher is average height and weight and wears a black vinyl raincoat. He never speaks. After exposing himself he simply leaves an index card with a short message before disappearing into the woods."

"So, Sherlock, what do you make of Primal Man's messages?"

"Well, Miss Marple, I would say that our perpetrator is a very frightened young man who is not doing well on the dating scene."

"No kidding! I'll bet you another dinner that Primal Man is one of George Savage's disciples."

"What leads you to that deduction, Detective Flores?"

"Come on, Hunter. Surely you know that Primal Man is the pseudonym that Savage uses to describe prehistoric man in his classes."

"I've heard that rumor."

Dinner arrived. After the usual chit-chat about how good the food smelled and looked, Graham resumed their conversation, "Maria, how come you are so interested in Savage?"

"I have a file on him. Savage's chauvinist ideology and sexist personal life are well-known around campus. I have interviewed a lot of his victims. I can't believe the campus administration continues to let him hide behind the cloak of academic freedom."

"Why haven't you written an article about him?"

"None of the victims filed complaints with the university or any government agency, and none of my sources will go on the record. So there is no story."

"Do you have anything that links Savage or one of his disciples directly to Primal Man?"

"No, just a journalist's intuition."

After considerable silence, Hunter spoke, "Maria, one of my officers is going to enroll in Savage's class, hoping to unmask Primal Man. I would also like to put some pressure on the professor. He may have some inkling as to who is masquerading as Primal Man. Would you be willing to help put the squeeze on him by sharing information from your files?"

"I can provide some information, but I won't reveal my sources without their permission."

"Understood."

"When do we get started?"

"How about at dinner this Friday?"

"Fine, but I don't think it would be good for either of our reputations to be seen cavorting in public. If you promise to behave and bring me a vegetarian pizza from Guido's, we can meet at my apartment. My files on Savage are there anyway."

"Maria, do I look like the kind of guy who would take advantage of a helpless journalist?"

"Yes, but I am hardly helpless."

Graham and Maria split the check as planned and walked slowly and silently through the Agora. Suddenly a Roma looking boy dressed in a white tunic and sandals appeared out of the darkness. He thrust a flyer advertising the services of the Delphi Oracle into Graham's hand. "Learn your future for only $25," he proclaimed. Graham tried to shoo the boy away, but Maria took a dollar from her purse and gave it to the child, thanking him for the flyer.

"Come on Graham, be a sport; let's consult the Oracle."

"What the hell! Even soothsayers need to earn a living."

"Don't be so cynical. My mother believed strongly in fortune tellers. She swore that she received better advice from these persecuted purveyors of truth than from her priest or her psychiatrist."

As they entered the temple Maria noted how ridiculous the two large Doric columns looked on such a small building. The priestess who explained the rules for interacting with the Oracle looked more Roma than Greek, but she played her part quite well. Maria volunteered to enter the sanctuary first. Rose scented vapors surrounded her. A mysterious voice with a foreign accent inquired,

"What knowledge do you seek from the Oracle?"

Maria playfully asked, "Is the Yanquee cop attracted to me?"

"Cupid has drawn his bow. He waits for the target to reveal herself."

Clever answer thought Maria as the attendant led her to the exit.

When Graham entered the inner sanctum the incense smell that rose from the floor reminded him of the funeral masses that he had attended as an altar boy. His musings were interrupted by a sympathetic voice,

"What wisdom do you seek from the Oracle?"

Graham smiled, "Will I make love to Maria Flores? "

"Love cannot be made. It can only be given."

The truth of that statement could never be challenged pondered Graham. With such prophecies this Oracle would remain in business a long time.

"Very interesting," proclaimed Graham as he joined Maria at the exit of the temple.

"What did you learn?"

"Maria, did you forget the warning of the priestess: 'Reveal the prophecy of the Oracle to no one, or risk the anger of the gods.'"

"Aha, has the great skeptic suddenly become a believer?"

"That's one possibility, or perhaps we officers of the law are afraid to break the rules."

"Or could it be that you cops clam up every time a reporter asks a question?"

"Equally plausible hypothesis."

"Okay, mystery man, walk me to my car."

An uncomfortable silence permeated the two-block journey to Maria's car. Graham felt like a self-conscious adolescent saying good-night to a girl on their first date. He subdued a crazy impulse to take Maria Flores into his arms and kiss her deeply. Instead he awkwardly muttered, "Um, thanks, Maria. I enjoyed tonight very much."

"Me too. See you tomorrow."

CHAPTER 9:
MARIA FLORES SEPTEMBER 30

As she drove home Maria Flores suddenly became aware of how attracted she was to Graham Hunter. He had stirred something inside her. She was surprised that a Yanquee, a cop no less, could have this effect on her. She knew Hunter was an honest and competent policeman, but until tonight she had always looked at him through her professional lens. Now her memory and imagination painted a portrait of him as a man. Large deep-set eyes were the windows to his feelings. As she replayed the evening she remembered the embarrassment unveiled in his eyes when she surprised him at the precinct; what was that all about she wondered? She remembered how preoccupied Graham looked at the beginning of dinner. However, when they were talking about Primal Man and George Savage, his indigo orbs displayed sensitivity and anger that gained her respect and trust. Then as they planned their next rendezvous his gaze became playful and mischievous. Finally, a few brief moments of incredible intensity, maybe even passion, were quickly followed by uncomfortable reticence as he said "good night."

Maria lit a vanilla scented candle, added lilac crystals to her bath, and put on her CD of Andean music. As she listened to the melancholic sounds of the quena, she continued to construct her portrait of the six foot, slightly overweight, Graham Hunter. She imagined herself stroking his wavy black hair and nibbling his neck. She fantasized being kissed by his thick full lips. As she slipped deeper into the bath bubbles her fingers began gentling rubbing her nipples until they were erect. Her right hand then drifted to her pubis and then to her clitoris. It was not a violent eruption, but rather a gradual build-up and slow release of sexual energy. Maria remained in the tub for another half hour savoring her imaginary tryst with the Yanquee policeman.

As she slipped into her flannel nightgown Maria's feelings toward Hunter overwhelmed her with anxiety. Was she really attracted to this cop? Why now? She tried to shrug off her bathtub orgasm to temporary horniness, but she knew that was a lie. For better or worse this shy gringo had stirred up something in her. Now what was she going to do? A professional partnership between a detective and a journalist was one thing, but a romantic relationship seemed like a recipe for disaster. Why was she obsessing about this? She didn't even know if he was available, or more importantly, interested in her. Sure he had flirted with her, but such overtures were hardly evidence of enduring interest. She wondered if Hunter had cleverly manipulated the whole situation in order to get an invitation to her apartment. Now Maria regretted having invited him for dinner. She worried that he would think she was coming on to him. Was he going to try to seduce her? Did she want him to?

"Ave Maria!" she screamed. "I don't need this. Why bring a man into my life now? Mother of God, make these feelings go away, and I will make a novena."

CHAPTER 10:
MARGO ELLY OCTOBER 1

Margo Elly's alarm sounded at 6:05 am, just as it had every day for the past twenty-five years. She promptly rose and began her morning routine: two minutes devoted to brushing teeth, ten minutes of stretching exercises, fifteen minutes on the treadmill, ten minutes for coffee and dry toast, a five minute cold shower, twelve minutes for dressing, and seven minutes for the drive to campus. Although she tried to rigorously stay on schedule, today was different. She and the president of the university would be holding a press conference announcing the establishment of the Margo Elly Fund for Women in Science. Elly had been granted a patent for a new contraceptive. She had decided to use her profits from the patent to establish a scholarship fund that would help women pursue careers in science at both the undergraduate and graduate level at Delphi University.

Margo arrived on campus five minutes late, having taken more than the allotted time to decide which silk scarf best complemented her blue suit. Nevertheless, if she hurried, she still had enough time to have her usual meeting with her graduate students to go over the results of the previous day's experiments before the press conference. She tried to focus on the computer output and the students' summary of the research, but not even iron-willed Margo Elly could contain her excitement. The Women in Science Fund was the culmination of her career. Her colleagues could no longer ignore her. She would be exalted by the faculty, students, and alumni of Delphi for all eternity. Margo and her chief research assistant, Judy Lacky, made their way across the courtyard to the steps of the administration building for the press conference. Margo's anticipatory exhilaration quickly turned to disappointment and anger when she saw the sparse attendance. Only two reporters were in the audience. None of her former students or her colleagues had bothered to attend. The President made a few perfunctory remarks thanking Elly for her generous gift and the impact it would have on future generations of women scientists at Delphi University. When it was Margo's turn to speak, she was so choked with rage and disillusionment that she forgot her prepared remarks. Her muffled voice uttered a barely audible, "Thank you. I am glad that I can contribute to the growth of women scientists." There were two questions about the size of the fund and how applicants would be chosen. The event was over in less than twenty minutes. Margo was devastated. Her dream of immortality had vaporized. Mechanically she walked toward her office. Judy Lacky tried to make conversation, but her mentor was oblivious to everyone and everything around her. Numbness temporarily dulled the burning sensation that had permeated her entire body during the press conference.

Margo spent the rest of the afternoon in her office shut off from the rest of the world. She tried to block out the memory of the morning events and revise a manuscript, but she could not maintain her focus. Images of the sparse crowd were too vivid and overwhelming. She also worried that Emily Smith would not take the Harvard fellowship. Even if Savage discarded her, Margo was not confident that her protégée would abandon her flirtation with evolutionary psychology.

That evening Margo sought sanctuary in the ritual of her bath, but the sitar music could not expel the memories of her encounter with George Savage and the press conference. Her cleansing sponges could not banish the negative feelings that invaded her like drug resistant bacteria. The scented bath water also provided no comfort; it only wrinkled her skin.

CHAPTER 11:
DONALD SPEAK OCTOBER 1

Donald Speak, Director of Communications at Delphi University, arrived early for the 7 pm emergency meeting of the cabinet. His boss, President Bertha Sinduce, sat stone-faced at the head of a large conference table in the Board Room. Her silver blue bouffant hair style was held firmly in place by massive amounts of hair spray. She appeared to be in a trance as she stared out her window at the Elysian Fields. This beautiful meadow of prairie grasses and wild flowers would one day be transformed into her dream, the Museum of Medicine (MOM). President Sinduce's mother had been the first woman to graduate from medical school in the state of Missouri. Sinduce wanted to build the museum to honor her mother for making it easier for future generations of women to enter the medical profession.

Speak had tried unsuccessfully to get his president to abandon the MOM project. He knew that the Faculty Senate opposed construction of the building. They argued that the university needed to take a leadership role in environmental conservation and preserve both the Elysian Fields and the Olympic Forest for posterity. The university could not expect local businesses and citizens to make sacrifices to preserve "America the Beautiful," if it did not conserve its own natural treasures. The faculty also thought it was ridiculous to build a museum dedicated to medicine on a campus that had no medical school. Finally, the faculty was concerned about both the capital and operating costs of the proposed museum. Such facilities always required ongoing subsidies to sustain them. The faculty was adamantly against reallocating funds from Delphi's small annual operating budget to support the egocentric dreams of President Sinduce.

Speak regretted the change in attitude that he had witnessed in Sinduce since she had been named the fifteenth president of Delphi

University. As a department chairperson and a dean Bertha Sinduce had a reputation as a consensus builder, an administrator who truly valued the ideas of the faculty. In fact, it was her reputation as the "good listener" that ultimately convinced the Board of Trustees to select her as the new president. However, once she seized power President Sinduce no longer heard the petitions of her faculty. There would be a MOM. Its opponents would be hushed or crushed.

Sinduce had entrusted fund raising for the building to her childhood friend, Liz Gold. Gold had been successful squeezing money from urban liberals, but her flashy bombastic style had raised little money from the more conservative parents of Delphi University. Most parents who sent their children to Delphi were not wealthy. Their only philanthropic contributions were to the Sunday collection box of their Church.

A campus crisis had necessitated the emergency meeting. Speak sat on the president's left constantly making notations in his spiral notebook. Liz Gold sat opposite him fussing with her teased platinum dyed hair. Campus Police Chief Robert Gunn stood at the other end of the table recounting the day's events.

"Witnesses report that at 9:50 am approximately one hundred female students assembled outside the large lecture hall in the Murky Social Science Building carrying signs that said "STOP PMS NOW." They then proceeded into the hall and disrupted Professor Savage's course on gender relationships. The demonstrators reportedly chanted the following slogan at a high volume, "Savage! Savage! You're a knave. You and Primal Man belong in a cave."

"Amen," interjected Liz Gold.

"Excuse me, Chief Gunn," interrupted Speak. "Why didn't your officers prohibit the demonstrators from entering the social science building and direct them to Freedom Square which has been designated the official protest area?"

"Donald, we had no advance warning. Once they were in the hall we did not want to risk a police-student confrontation."

Irritated President Sinduce glared at Speak and Gold. "Let Chief Gunn finish his presentation. There will be plenty of time for questions and explanations later."

"Thank you, Madame President. At approximately 3 pm ten male students interrupted a meeting of the Women's Studies Program in the

Anthony Conference Room shouting, "German, German! You're no fun. You dykes had better run."

"There's some truth to that," interjected Gold.

"Control yourself, Liz," scolded President Sinduce. "Continue, Chief."

"One of the janitors called campus police when he saw the confrontation. My officers responded in approximately ten minutes. The officers witnessed no violence—only a lot of shouting between the two groups. Lieutenant Baton ordered the male students to disperse."

"Anything else, Chief?"

"Not at this time. Baton is interviewing both groups to learn more about these incidents and any other planned actions."

Sinduce turned to Gold and Speak, "Any questions for the Chief?"

"Chief, were there any video or other cameras present at either of these events?" asked Speak.

"I don't believe so."

Seeing that there were no other questions President Sinduce dismissed Gunn. Then she turned toward Speak, "What now, Donald?"

"No pictures are a good omen. The television stations may not even mention the incident. There will be a story in the newspaper tomorrow, but with no photos it won't make the front page. The problem for you, Madame President, is to prevent this from spreading. If the two warring factions get organized and tip-off the media about planned actions, there will be pictures and then we have a whole new ball game. If some reporter starts linking these demonstrations with the campus flasher, we have even more problems. Parents start worrying about campus security and enrollments decline."

"This is going to screw up my whole capital campaign," whined Liz Gold. "Bertha, I can't raise money for the Museum of Medicine with this going on. Donors don't like campus controversies."

"Any suggestions for ending this mess?" asked Sinduce.

"Fire both of them!" screeched Gold in disgust.

Very deliberately Sinduce turned toward Gold and placed her index finger over her tightly closed lips like a spinster school marm scolding a talkative pupil. Exasperated she looked to Speak for help. "Donald, do you have a more realistic solution given that both German and Savage have tenure?"

"Under the circumstances I recommend bribery."

"Explain yourself, Donald."

"I would begin by inviting Professor Savage for a sympathetic chat. You can tell him how supportive of academic freedom you are and how disappointed you were in the action of the female students. To alleviate this stressful situation for him, you are willing to offer him an immediate paid leave to pursue his research in Africa on the origins of Primal Man. With Savage gone, German will not have a visible target for her campaign against the Program in Male Studies. The demonstrations will stop."

"And what if Savage refuses the paid leave?"

"I don't think he will. He has the reputation of being a real hedonist. However, if he does, then you can make the same offer to German. She hasn't had a leave in ten years. She would be delighted to spend a semester in her beloved England researching the love lives of the Bronte sisters."

"Thanks, Donald. I'll call Savage this evening."

The president concluded the meeting and exhaled deeply. She asked Speak to remain. After the other members had left she turned toward Speak and vented her frustration over recent events. Sinduce could not fathom what motivated a college boy to expose his privates to campus co-eds. The boy must be extremely disturbed to disgrace himself in such a way. Her most intense disgust, however, was reserved for the campus radicals. Why couldn't they have delayed their war until after the MOM had been built?

Speak tried to comfort his boss and friend by reminding her of her past successes in mediating campus conflicts, but the president was fed up. She had waited thirty years for this moment. She no longer had the patience to bargain with the faculty about anything, particularly the construction of the MOM. She also told Speak that if Gold did not raise ten million dollars soon, she was going to dismiss her and hire someone who could raise the money.

Speak left the campus with a heavy heart. He had failed to convince Sinduce to negotiate with the faculty about the MOM. Moreover, his good friend, Liz Gold, was likely to be fired. He also feared for his own job security. President Sinduce had concluded their meeting by reminding him that it was his responsibility as communications director to stop the bad publicity. He knew that assignment was nearly impossible. It took a half bottle of scotch before he could fall asleep.

CHAPTER 12:
GRAHAM HUNTER OCTOBER 2

Hunter was halfway through his third cup of coffee and his second donut when he spotted the following story on page 12 of the news paper.

> Yesterday two campus demonstrations disrupted the usual tranquility of Delphi University. In the morning one hundred female students demonstrated outside the class of Anthropology Professor George Savage. Approximately ten male students staged a counter-demonstration at a meeting of the Women's Studies Program in the afternoon. No injuries were reported according to campus police. Director of University Communications, Donald Speak, was unable to identify the sponsor of either demonstration.

Kevin O'Rourke, accompanied by Kathy O'Malley, knocked lightly on the door and entered Hunter's office.

"Graham, I assume you saw the article in today's paper. Both of us were at the demonstrations yesterday."

Hunter nodded affirmatively and motioned for the two young police officers to be seated. "How was it that you two campus radicals ended up at the demonstrations?"

"I was attending my first class with Professor Savage," reported O'Rourke.

"Pure serendipity," explained O'Malley. "I was on my way to my criminal investigation class and I heard the ruckus. My contempt for Savage compelled me to hang around and watch the action. Then my police instincts kicked in. I befriended another student who told me about the afternoon meeting."

"Can either of you tell me anything more than the Scribe?"

O'Rourke spoke first. "Savage was giving a lecture in his course, 'Gender Relationships: Biological Destiny.' He looked like he had just awoken from a horrendous drunk. His eyes were bloodshot; his hair was uncombed; his clothes were disheveled; and he was sweating profusely. Half way through the lecture approximately one hundred women paraded down the aisle carrying signs that read, 'STOP PMS NOW.' Then they stopped in front of the stage and started chanting, 'Savage! Savage! You're a knave. You and Primal Man belong in a cave.' Savage turned up the volume on the speaker and tried to continue the lecture, but he could not compete with the screaming co-eds. After ten minutes he threw up his arms and stomped off the stage. The demonstrators clapped their hands and pumped their fists in victory."

"Officer O'Malley, any idea who organized the event?"

"One of the students told me that Dr. German, Director of the Women's Studies Program, ordered the demonstration against Savage. She blames him and PMS for creating the campus flasher. The fact he calls himself 'Primal Man' makes her argument pretty credible."

"Kevin, any leads on the identity of Primal Man?"

"No. I did talk with some of Savage's students. They are pissed at German, but they are equally angry at Primal Man for discrediting Savage. None of my informants was willing to venture a guess about the identity of the flasher."

"Okay, let's keep with our current plan then. Kevin, you keep hanging around Savage's disciples. Kathy, I appreciate your input, but you are not officially on this case. Your supervisor may not appreciate your moonlighting, so for the time being I recommend that you cease your inquires."

"Excuse me, sir. Primal Man has really frightened the women of Delphi University. You need to catch him soon. If you need someone to work undercover, I would like to volunteer."

"Thanks, Kathy. I appreciate your willingness to help."

After the two young officers left, Graham grabbed a tennis ball from his bottom drawer and began bouncing it off the wall and catching it as he paced back and forth in his office. He frequently engaged in this ritualistic behavior when he was stumped. There was no evidence that the tennis ball compulsion had ever helped him solve a crime, but the scarred walls in his office provided abundant data regarding the frequency of his brain freezes. After fifteen minutes of tortured exercise and meditation, Hunter collapsed in his chair and washed the remaining donut remnant down with cold coffee.

CHAPTER 13:
MARGO ELLY OCTOBER 2

A week had past since the debacle of the sparsely attended press conference, but Margo Elly was still angry and hurt. She had fervently believed that the Women in Science Scholarship Program would guarantee her immortality. The *Delphi Scribe* had only run a brief story on page 38 about her largess. Had all of her hard work been in vain? Her legacy seemed very much in doubt. Adding insult to injury Emily Smith was nowhere to be found. She had simply stopped coming to the lab. Margo felt like she had lost all control of her life. She had a difficult time getting out of bed and ate very little. At the office she was no longer able to concentrate on her own work. She exhibited even less interest in the research findings of her students. Judy Lacky was now forced to make all of the decisions in the lab.

Some days Margo felt so bad that she didn't leave the house. Today was one of those days. She remained in the safety of her bed until noon. For two hours she sat on her couch in her pajamas staring at lab reports of her research on "Passion with Protection," a spermicide that also increased libido. She had been convinced that this new drug would bring her everlasting fame, but now she doubted that it would ever come to market. Demoralized Margo threw the lab reports across the room. After three glasses of chardonnay she fell soundly asleep on the couch. It was 6 pm before she forced herself to move. Dinner consisted of unheated, left-over lasagna and more wine. Two hours of *I Love Lucy* reruns were insufficient to put her to sleep.

Desperate for help she slipped her track suit over her pajamas and slowly made her way to the Temple of the Oracle. Mechanically she gave her $25 to the priestess and entered the sanctuary. The aroma that rose from the grates smelled like a funeral parlor. A comforting voice beckoned her to bare her soul.

"What guidance do you seek from the Oracle, my child?"

"Will I ever become famous?"

"Yes, fame will be your companion for eternity."

The prophecy provided no comfort for Margo Elly. Dejected she made her way home. She shed her track suit and prepared her ritual bath. The numbing sounds of the sitar filled the room as she sat at her vanity brushing her hair, but after only a few strokes she abandoned the sacred rite. As the water gently cascaded over her unshaven legs she renewed her skin with her sponges. Once the cleansing ritual was completed she slid down into the tub until her entire body was covered with rose scented bath bubbles. Unfortunately, the healing power of her purification rite diminished almost as soon as she stepped from the tub. Margo's feelings of rejection and failure resurfaced almost immediately. She felt trapped. Lethargically she climbed into bed and began reading *Between the Acts* by Virginia Woolf until sleep provided a temporary reprieve from her melancholy.

CHAPTER 14:
GRAHAM HUNTER OCTOBER 3

"Rape is an evolutionary necessity and so is the Program in Male Studies." Hunter read this latest message from Primal Man for the third time hoping to gain some insight into the mind of the campus flasher. However, there was no telepathic communication between the exhibitionist and the detective. The description of Primal Man provided by the most recent casualty was identical to that of previous victims—same costume, mute, average height and weight. However, there was one disturbing difference in the most recent attack. The flasher had been less timid in his interaction with his prey. He had spent several minutes angrily stroking his neon orange weapon before making his escape. This new behavior and the more threatening message worried Hunter. He feared that Primal Man might physically assault his next victim.

Just as Hunter was finishing a memo asking his supervisor for permission to have Kathy O'Malley work undercover, Justin Mather, the county prosecutor, blew into his office like a tornado. Mather looked possessed; the man's eyes never blinked.

"Hunter, you have to do something about the lawlessness that has overtaken Delphi University. We can't let that pervert keep exposing himself to good Christian women. When are you going to catch the faggot?"

"Sir, we actually don't know the sexual orientation of the perpetrator."

"Don't get smart with me, boy! You had better arrest someone soon, or I will have your badge."

"Don't try to bully me, Justin. I'm not terribly worried about my job security. Now let's try to act civilized. I have several officers working on the case, but so far we have no concrete leads."

"Find him soon, Graham. Anyone who gets his jollies out of scaring women with his pecker ain't all there and that makes him dangerous."

"I will do my best, sir."

"Now, what are you going to do about those lesbian hussies demonstrating all over town?"

"Absolutely nothing, Justin. Remember the first amendment."

"Boy, one of these days, that smart mouth of yours is going to cost you your job."

"Justin, go back to your office and let me do my job."

Mather had become a constant irritant since his election as county prosecutor six months ago. The 6' 4" prosecutor had the girth of a sequoia and the intelligence of an ant. His untamed burnt orange hair matched his volatile emotional disposition. Worse yet he possessed the same intolerant attitudes and beliefs of his distant ancestor, the fire and brimstone preacher Cotton Mather.

Hunter spent the next six hours wandering through the campus of Delphi University. He didn't know what else to do. Perhaps by visiting the scenes of the flashing incidents he would somehow mystically receive some intuitive insight into Primal Man's character. As he walked through the campus quad and wandered through the buildings, a frustrating, but relentless idea, seized' control of his mind. He had probably walked right past Primal Man; perhaps he had even said hello to him. He started looking intently into the eyes of all the males who passed by, magically hoping that somehow he would uncover the flasher's identity. After several hours of failing to ferret out Primal Man with his sixth sense, Graham decided to rely on more conventional investigative methods and made his way to the office of Chief Gunn.

Gunn was as officious as ever. His reports were as bland as the man himself. Intuitive and creative were two adjectives that had never been used to describe him. Nor would anyone accuse him of being spontaneous or mercurial. Cold, rigid, and dull were words that captured the essence of Gunn. After ten minutes of polite nothingness Graham knew that he was wasting his time. Either Gunn was holding back information, or he knew less about what was going on at Delphi University than Hunter did. Graham suspected the latter.

By the time Graham reached home he realized that he was totally confused. What was he thinking meandering around campus like some lost teenager? He had not even been wise enough to interview any of the students that he had passed during his misguided pilgrimage. After gulping down some Kentucky Fried Chicken, he secured a bottle of Newcastle ale and plopped down in his favorite recliner. Tonight he wanted to explore the forces that drove Primal Man. Why had he chosen to promote the ideology of the sociobiologists by exposing himself to Delphi co-eds?

In Graham's view existentialism, of all the philosophical systems, had the most to say about man's need to find meaning in the world. Sartre placed great emphasis on being-for-itself. Man is not a passive actor; he acts upon the world and he refuses to be simply defined by his roles in society or the perspective of others. This active use of man's freedom leads the self and others to examine the motives behind his actions. Graham was especially drawn to this view of man's place in the universe. He no longer believed that the deity had a plan for him or for any of his fellow human beings. Each person came into this world essentially alone. Thus, in their own bumbling way all individuals had to create their own purposeful life.

Graham wondered where Primal Man was in his search for a meaningful existence. What system of values, if any, had his parents tried to inculcate in him? Had they encouraged him to be his own man, or had they rigidly tried to mold him in their own images? Something in Primal Man's family must have gone terribly wrong for him to be so desperate to be seen and heard, but why had he chosen the PMS to express himself? Unfortunately, without interacting with him the detective had little hope of answering any of these existential questions.

CHAPTER 15:
PRIMAL MAN OCTOBER 3

Once again Primal Man had made the front page of the Delphi Scribe. He wished that he could share his latest victory with his father. His dad would be proud of him for standing up to the feminists. He had shown them who was in charge. Now every woman on campus would fear and respect him.

Primal Man's father had never been able to challenge the women in his life, particularly his wife and his boss. Two years ago he finally succumbed to their relentless attacks and simply vanished. No one knew where he had sought refuge. A year before his disappearance he had lost his job driving a delivery truck for a bread company. His female supervisor claimed that he was terminated for excessive absences and too many accidents. He maintained that he was fired because he was a man. He alleged that the manager was a lesbian who was systematically replacing all of the male drivers with her fellow dykes.

Primal Man's mother was hardly supportive of her husband. She called him a bigot and a loser. The shouting matches between his parents became more frequent and intense as the years dragged on. His mother was forever abandoning the family and locking herself in what was now her bedroom. His father sought solace in the bottle. Primal Man and his kid sister tried to escape the war between their parents by sequestering themselves in the family room and turning up the volume on the TV. At bedtime they prayed the rosary together.

College had not provided any respite from the relentless attacks of women upon his manhood. These hussies used their bodies and their glib tongues to win the favor of the teachers. In social situations these vamps would titillate, but they would not put out (at least not for him). However, when he was Primal Man he was in control; the bitches had to respect him. Unfortunately, this feeling of power did not last long after he returned to his civilian status. His Catholicism would not let him accept the gospel of the PMS without question. He was conflicted. After he recited the rosary he prayed to another warrior, St. Michael, for guidance.

CHAPTER 16:
MARIA FLORES, OCTOBER 4

Maria Flores had been unable to concentrate all day. She was as nervous as a school girl about her dinner with Graham Hunter. She felt compelled to clean her apartment before the detective arrived. Half way through changing the sheets on the bed, it dawned on her that she was preparing for a date rather than a business meeting. "What am I doing? she screamed. Nevertheless, she went ahead and finished putting the new satin sheets on the bed. However, she decided to change her outfit. She replaced the mini-skirt and low-cut blouse with jeans and a turtleneck. Her Carolina Herrera perfume remained; it was too expensive to waste. Then she removed the candles from the dining room table—not appropriate for a business meeting. Bach replaced Sinatra on the stereo, and the doorbell rang.

After exchanging greetings, Maria took the pizza from Hunter and directed him to the dining room table. When she returned, Maria could tell that something was wrong. Graham had a frown on his face and his eyes definitely had the look of a troubled man.

"What's wrong?" she asked.

"Primal Man struck again and his message was much more threatening." Hunter then quoted the latest communiqué from the flasher.

"This exhibitionist is dangerous, Graham. Harmless pranksters don't use the word 'rape' in their communications. What are you going to do?"

"I requested permission for one of the female officers to work undercover. Maybe we will get lucky and Primal Man will choose the wrong woman to assault."

"I certainly hope so."

During the remainder of the meal Maria noticed that when they were not talking about business Graham had difficulty maintaining eye contact with her and his conversation became stilted. She concluded that the confident policeman became an introvert when he was not in his professional role. Taking pity on the reticent cop, shy asked him a work related question. "Graham, are you ready to look at my files on Savage?"

"Ready."

Graham cleared the table while Maria retrieved the files. Maria motioned for the detective to sit next to her. "Hunter, remember your promise. All of my sources are confidential."

"Agreed."

Slowly and deliberately Maria untied the accordion style folder and cautiously handed it to Graham. He lifted the flap which revealed four files. Hunter began with Savage's police record. There were ten DWI's from five different states. In addition, a clipping from the Biloxi Herald described how a drunken Savage had killed a black woman and her unborn child in a horrendous automobile crash. A follow-up story in the Nation of Islam Messenger berated the white Biloxi prosecutor for plea bargaining the case. The original manslaughter charge had been reduced to a DWI. "Bastard," uttered Hunter as he closed the file.

The "marital history" file contained information on Savage's four ex-wives. All of them had been former students of Savage and considerably younger. None of the marriages had lasted more than three years; nor had they produced any children. The "other victims" file contained information on ten students who had been sexually harassed in some way by Savage. Maria explained that most of the victims were under twenty-one. Most of the students were flattered and consented to his advances; only later did they realize that they had been used. A few were married and should have known better, but they were in bad marriages and vulnerable to the attention Savage gave them. Now they were angry and ashamed. The two women who had rejected his advances paid with bad grades.

"Did these last two file a grievance against Savage through the university?"

"No, a counselor advised against it. Savage only gives essay tests, so it's nearly impossible to prove that you got a bad grade because you wouldn't put out."

The "macho garbage" file contained copies of the syllabi to Savage's courses, copies of his reprints, as well as articles by other proponents of evolutionary psychology and sociobiology. The titles of the articles were provocative and disgusting: "An evolutionary justification for rape," "Polygamy and survival of the fittest," "Sex and aggression: Nature's way," and "The importance of infidelity in improving the gene pool."

"Maria, I don't have the stomach to read this trash now, but I would like copies."

"I thought you might." Maria handed him a large manila envelope labeled, "Evolution Gone Wrong."

With that exchange Graham and Maria decided to call it a night. As Hunter walked down the sidewalk Maria lingered at the window until the shy gringo got into his car. Once again, she invoked the Virgin Mother, "Ave Maria, I begged you not to let this happen! I don't want this! It's going to make me crazy!" But Maria knew it was too late. The Yanquee cop had already touched her soul. The only remaining question was: Would he be touching her body? Mechanically she returned all of the documents to their designated place in the accordion file folder and hid it in her bedroom closet. Then she turned on the CD player and drew her bath. Tonight Tchaikovsky's Violin Concerto and the smell of lavender would provide the atmosphere for her fantasy rendezvous with the gringo with indigo eyes.

CHAPTER 17:
GRAHAM HUNTER OCTOBER 4

When he returned home Graham reflected on the day's events. He had been distracted the entire day. Images and thoughts of Maria Flores kept interrupting his work. He had both dreaded and looked forward to his meeting with her. The physical attraction that he felt was obvious, but there was something else about this Chilean journalist. She was clearly a feminist, but she wasn't above flirting. She was serious, but not humorless. However, it was her passion that most excited the stoic Graham—not just her commitment to finding truth and righting wrongs, but her enthusiasm for life in general. He remembered the sigh of ecstasy that she exuded when she tasted her first bite of mousaka, and the exhilaration that emanated from her when she grabbed his arm and pointed to the harvest moon. Did her passion extend to him, however? He was confident that Maria *liked* him, but did she *want* him. He wasn't ready to risk rejection.

When he had entered Maria's apartment he felt the same social ineptness that he had felt at the Parthenon. Twice he had to resort to the beet trick to keep his lust under control. Hunter didn't have a clue regarding Maria's feelings toward him; it was driving him crazy. The Savage discussion had provided a momentary respite from his fixation with Maria Flores, but the Chilean goddess dominated his thoughts during the drive home. He couldn't concentrate. His mind kept jumping from one topic to another, and his emotions were changing equally fast. One moment he would be thinking about Savage, and he could feel his stomach tighten and his face become flushed. Then he would see Maria Flores, more vulnerable than he had ever seen her. He wanted to hold her and protect her. Then the images of Savage's battered wives obliterated Maria's countenance and he felt intense rage.

After arriving home and checking the mail, he put on his Roberta Flack CD. When Roberta sang, "The first time ever I saw your face . . . ," Maria Flores appeared. Once again they were having dinner at the Parthenon. She was wearing the red knit jersey that accented her perfect breasts. No man could ignore her slim waste and cute butt that were covered, but not hidden, by her figure hugging black jeans. Her long, thick, raven hair was tied back and secured with an ornate comb from a past era. Her brown eyes sparkled with mischief and curiosity. Maria's image was quickly replaced by a hideous, serpentine creature with Savage's lecherous face. The creature laughed malevolently as he roughly fondled three women who were bound and gagged. First the faces of the women reminded Hunter of the photos he had seen in Maria's apartment, but then they morphed into images of his sisters. Graham turned off the CD player; there was no point in trying to restart his fantasy rendezvous with his favorite journalist. Savage had seized his mind. There was nothing else to do but delve into "Evolution Gone Wrong."

BOOK TWO

DEATH COMES TO DELPHI

Man can will nothing unless he has first understood that he must count on no one but himself; that he is alone, abandoned on earth in the midst of his infinite responsibilities, without help, with no other aim than the one he sets himself, with no other destiny than the one he forges for himself on this earth. (Jean-Paul Sartre)

I put for the general inclination of all mankind, a perpetual and restless desire of power after power, that ceaseth only in death. (Thomas Hobbs)

CHAPTER 18:
GRAHAM HUNTER OCTOBER 7

Hunter arrived at the crime scene at 1:40 pm as the medical examiner was completing his initial evaluation of the body in the kitchen. The woman's mouth was covered with duct tape and her arms were spread crucifixion style. Her wrists were secured with handcuffs to barstools that anchored the ends of a work table in the center of the kitchen. The victim appeared to have been sexually assaulted. Her t-shirt had been sliced open; each small breast bore fang-like cuts crusted with blood. The victim's black lace panties had also been slashed with a sharp object. Her legs and torso were bruised in many places. A small souvenir baseball bat, autographed by Stan Musial, lay next to her. Glass shards from a broken wine bottle and two glasses were scattered on the floor. Hunter told the technicians to bag the large pieces of glass, so that they could be dusted for finger prints.

Hunter looked up from the victim and was immediately struck by the strange juxtaposition of the messy crime scene on the floor against the incredible order in the rest of the kitchen. There were no dirty dishes in the sink or on the counters. All of the appliances were immaculate, not a speck of dirt or grease anywhere. Everything had a designated place. The pans were carefully arranged by size on hooks above the range. Coffee mugs were neatly organized on a shelf above the coffee maker. In the open pantry canned goods were arranged in precise rows by product. Unlike most modern kitchens the refrigerator was devoid of the clutter of notes and photos suspended by magnets. Instead a message board was hung on the wall near the phone. A marking pen and cleaning rag were conveniently attached.

The medical examiner interrupted the detective's scanning of the kitchen. "The victim has been dead about twelve hours, Graham. She appears to have been sexually assaulted, but until I examine her I won't know the full extent of her internal injuries. I didn't see any obvious evidence of semen or pubic hair other than that of the victim, but the lab reports will tell us for sure. As you can see, there is little blood. There are no obvious head wounds. Although there are numerous bruises on her legs and abdomen, none of them appear severe enough to have killed her. Until I do an autopsy I cannot speculate on the cause of death."

Graham turned to Detective O'Rourke who had preceded him at the scene. "Have you ID'd the victim yet, Kevin?"

"Her name is Margo Elly. She is a professor at Delphi University."

"Who called the police?"

"Her husband, Mr. Michael Hammer. He says he discovered the body about 1 pm when he returned after a week-end visit to his parents' home in Chicago. He claims that he called the police immediately and touched nothing but the phone."

"Any sign of forced entry?'

"No."

"Anything else, Kevin?"

"Not yet. I only arrived fifteen minutes ago."

"Okay, you finish interviewing the first responders. Then talk to the neighbors to see if they heard or saw anything. I will meet you at the office at 7 am tomorrow morning. We won't have anything from forensics before then anyway. I am going to make a quick trip over to the university to see Father Dominic. He may know the victim. At the very least he can make some suggestions regarding whom to question. Now I am going to talk to Mr. Hammer and take a tour of Dr. Elly's home."

"Graham, do you think that Primal Man has graduated from flashing to murder?"

"It's a possibility, but let's not jump to conclusions. See you in the morning."

Mike Hammer was about 5' 8", overweight, slovenly dressed, with a greasy complexion. He was staring at a wedding photograph on the mantle of the fireplace.

"Mr. Hammer, I am Detective Hunter. Please accept my condolences. We will do everything we can to catch the person who killed your wife. I know that you talked briefly to Detective O'Rourke, but I need to ask you a few more questions. Now think carefully and tell me what you saw when you arrived home this afternoon."

"When I saw Margo's car in the drive-way, I thought she must be sick. She never takes off work. I unlocked the door and called for her, but there was no response. Then I got nervous. I set my suitcase down and went into the kitchen. That's when I saw her lying on the floor. I knew that she was dead. Her face was so white; blood was congealed on her breasts; and she looked so rigid."

"Do you know of any enemies that your wife might have had?"

"No."

"Had she seemed worried or upset about anything lately?"

"Not that I could tell."

"Does the autographed bat that was found next to your wife belong to you?"

"Yes."

"Mr. Hammer, how long does it take you to drive from Chicago to Delphi?"

"About five and a half hours."

"And what time did you leave Chicago this morning?"

"Around eight in the morning."

"Can anyone verify that?"

"I doubt it. My parents went to work before I left. Am I a suspect?"

"Right now everyone is a suspect. If I were you, I would try to find someone who can confirm that you were in Chicago until 8 am. Finally, I am going to ask you to stay somewhere else for the next few days. We will seal the premises with police tape until the technicians have finished. No one should enter the house until the police remove the yellow tape. Do you need to get anything before you leave?"

"No, I'll just wash the clothes that I have in my suitcase. My shaving kit is there, so I'm fine. I just want to get out of this house as soon as possible. It gives me the creeps right now."

"I understand. Here is my card. Call me later with a phone number where I can reach you?"

After Mike Hammer had left, Hunter put on his latex gloves to begin his inspection of the crime scene. As he stepped into the living room he closed his eyes. He wanted to learn as much about the victim as possible by injecting himself into her environment. He knew his immersion technique was not textbook forensics, but he felt that he could learn something about the victim by quietly using all of his senses. He inhaled deeply, but the room was absent of smell.

Hunter opened his eyes. Floor to ceiling book cases covered all of the available wall space. The books appeared to be arranged alphabetically by category. There were a few art and history books, but most were novels or anthologies of short-stories. Crime mysteries dominated the collection. Agatha Christie, P.D. James, and Stuart Kaminsky were particularly well represented. A phone, a single pen, and a message pad were neatly arranged on a small writing table in one corner of the room. The seating area in front of the fireplace consisted of three forest green love seats arranged around an oriental rug with a burgundy background. The end tables and reading lamps at the junctions of the love seats reinforced the impression that the room was designed more for solitary reading than entertaining. On one of the end tables was the *"Awakening"* by Kate Chopin.

The dining room was sterile and sparsely furnished with a chrome and glass table, a matching side table, and six black leather upholstered chairs that looked very uncomfortable. A manila folder containing two articles from the popular men's magazine *"Man: the Hunter"* lay on the side-table. The first article was entitled, "What evolutionary biology tells us about gender relationships." The author was none other than, George Savage. The second article, "Sex and Snakes," had been written by another professor at Delphi University, Jacob Spearman. Hunter placed the file folder in an evidence bag.

The bathroom was immaculate and multi-scented. It was a 1930s style bathroom with an off-white ceramic floor. Ivory tiles with black accents on the top and bottom rows covered the lower half of the wall. A small alcove contained a built-in vanity of black slate and a mirror with art deco lighting. A hair brush with no stray hair and a basket of potpourri occupied the corners of the vanity table. A drawer beneath the table contained lipstick and other make-up precisely arranged. The waste basket under the vanity was empty. In the medicine cabinet a single toothbrush, toothpaste, Vaseline, four types of pain killers, and three types of laxatives were carefully arranged on the spotless shelves. The linen closet was yet another example of regimented order. One shelf contained toilet paper in four straight rows. Bath oils were on a second shelf, arranged by scent. A third shelf contained the towels and washcloths which were folded precisely with no uneven edges. Cleaning supplies were arranged in neat rows on the floor of the closet. Sponges of all different shapes and textures were placed neatly in the corners of the bathtub. Rose scented bath gel, rather than a bar of soap, occupied the soap dish. A book of crossword puzzles and a can of air freshener (mountain breeze) adorned the toilet tank. Hunter surmised that Margo Elly spent a lot of time in this room.

A bedroom was the only remaining room on the first floor. It too was a paragon of order and cleanliness. An Indian print bedspread covered a queen size bed; the pillows were fluffed just so. An alarm clock and a small lamp sat on the night stand. Hunter opened the drawer of the night stand which contained a vibrator, a dildo, a tube of KY jelly and a book entitled, *How to Love Yourself*. Good illustrations, thought Hunter, as he flipped through this woman's guide to masturbation. A small bowl of dried flowers adorned the chest of drawers at the other end of the room. The top drawer contained bras and panties, lined up in precise rows. Socks and nylons were carefully aligned in the next drawer. The third drawer contained t-shirts, ironed and neatly folded. In the bottom drawer were sweaters in vinyl bags. The closet also was a masterpiece of organization with one pole for dresses, two hangers (upper and lower) for blouses and slacks, and a shoe rack on the floor.

Hunter climbed the stairs to the second floor. The moldy smell of male sweat permeated the air. A set of golf clubs and golf shoes lay on the floor of the hall. Straight ahead was a bathroom. Several grungy towels and dirty underwear were strewn on the floor. Hair from every part of the body was stuck to sink, shower, toilet, and floor. You could hardly see yourself in the mirror due to the splatter from years of careless tooth brushing and rinsing. The shelves of the medicine cabinet contained a razor, shaving cream, cheap aftershave, several types of antacid, a huge bottle of aspirin, and several layers of dirt.

Off to Hunter's left was a small bedroom. It contained a twin bed, a chest of drawers, and a small night stand. Dirty clothes were scattered everywhere. All of the drawers of the chest were open, and dirty dishes were stacked on top. The bed was not made and the sheets were covered with food stains. There was no order in the closet either. Work clothes and dress clothes were intermingled in random fashion;

unpaired sneakers, soccer cleats, and dress shoes were piled in a corner. Hunter labeled the odor in this room, "primitive bachelor."

Another bedroom functioned as a den. A 32" TV was in one corner of the room; in the opposite corner was a recliner and a small coffee table that was home to an open bag of potato chips and several empty beer cans. Piles of magazines were thrown haphazardly on the floor near the recliner. The collection was primarily sports oriented, but there were also several pornographic magazines. Hunter wiped off the recliner and carefully inspected the magazine evidence. The owner was clearly a heterosexual male who preferred big breasted women who did not shave their privates.

The last room had been converted into a make-shift kitchen. A small table with a single chair was along one wall. There was a small refrigerator which contained only beer, milk, and soda. A metal cabinet contained a few dishes and some silverware; a hot plate, coffee maker, and toaster were on top. The closet had been converted into a sparse pantry. Boxes of cereal and macaroni and cheese were on the top shelf; cans of soup, corn beef hash, ravioli, and spam were on another shelf.

Hunter shook his head in amazement as he walked down the stairs. Margo Elly and Mike Hammer were the married equivalent of the "Odd Couple." It appeared that they spent most of their time living on separate floors. How did the marriage survive? pondered Hunter.

The body of Margo Elly had been taken to the morgue, but the lab technicians were still dusting for finger prints, taking photographs, and looking for other evidence. Hunter found the steps to the basement and descended. On the right was the laundry room. The cleanliness and order suggested that this room was the exclusive territory of Margo Elly. Off to the left was a small room which was locked. Using his lock pick Hunter was able to open it easily. The room contained only a double bed and a large trunk. The trunk was also locked, but the padlock was easily picked. Inside were the love-making devices used in bondage: leather handcuffs, a spiked dog collar, a whip, ankle restraints, a black leather corset with garters, black mesh nylons, black high heels, and a black leather jockstrap. Hunter now had at least one possible explanation for the survival of the marriage of Margo Elly and Mike Hammer. He couldn't help but notice that this room was different from the other places in which Margo Elly had lived. The stale air, swollen with mold and dust, nearly choked him. The tile floor, bed, and trunk were covered with layers of dust, and cobwebs dangled precariously from the ceiling. Margo Elly could not have tolerated being in this unclean place, no matter how great the sensual pleasure. This love nest had not been visited by her in quite some time.

Returning to the living room Graham once again tried to bond with the victim in her habitat. He sat on the cushion which seemed to have the most wear. Graham closed his eyes, hoping to learn more about Margo Elly by literally sitting in her place. He was unable to visualize anything, but he felt extremely isolated and lonely. He wondered if she had felt the same way.

After checking one last time with the lab technicians, Graham left for Father Dominic's. When Dom opened the door and saw the worried look on his friend's face, he knew this was not a social call. "What's wrong, Graham? Has Primal Man flashed his weenie again?"

"Much more serious than that, Dom. Professor Elly has been murdered?"

Hunter described the crime scene in such grisly detail that Dom finally held up his hands and pleaded, "Enough, Graham, I've got the picture."

"So, Dom, what can you tell me about Dr. Elly?"

"She was Professor of Biochemistry and Women's Studies. She recently received a patent for a new female contraceptive. She is donating her profits from the patent to establish a scholarship program to encourage women to pursue careers in science."

"Sounds like a wonderful human being. Who would want to murder her?"

"I imagine that Dr. Elly had a lot of enemies. She had a reputation for being a difficult person. Students were always complaining to me about how unfair she was."

"Can you narrow the list of suspects, Dom?"

"There are two male faculty members for whom she had personal vendettas. First, there is Jacob Spearman. He was a notorious womanizer. Finally, the inevitable happened; one of his victims, with Elly's support, filed sexual harassment charges. He could have escaped with a warning for a first time offense, but Dr. Elly convinced two other victims to also file complaints. The president, with the support of the university lawyers, gave Spearman an ultimatum: resign or be fired. He is now working as a salesman for Jones Medical Supply—a brilliant career down the toilet because he couldn't control his urges. Stupid!"

"Did he know that Dr. Elly was behind his ouster?"

"Sure, everyone did."

"Do you know if Spearman ever threatened Dr. Elly?"

"Can't help you there, Graham."

"Okay, who was Dr. Elly's other enemy?"

"Your friend, George Savage. One of Elly's research assistants, Emily Smith, became involved with Savage. Emily has received a fellowship to study biochemistry at Harvard next year, but she was considering declining it to spend next year with Savage. Dr. Elly was furious."

"How do you know about this, Dom?"

"Emily came to see me last week. She was raised in a very Catholic family; two brothers are priests and a sister is a nun. Her family never forgave her for abandoning her Catholic roots to attend a secular university. Until recently biochemistry had replaced her *Baltimore Catechism* as the authoritative source for answers to life's questions. Then she became smitten with Savage and sociobiology. Now she is terribly conflicted about everything. Emily believed that Dr. Elly had some kind of confrontation with Savage, but she did not know any details. Please try to leave her out of this. She's gone home to be with her family while she sorts out what she wants to do with her life. I am sure that she prefers to keep her involvement with Savage a secret from her parents."

"Okay, I will start with Savage, but I may have to interview Ms. Smith eventually."

"I understand. Graham, you should also interview Elly's research assistants; she spent a lot of time in her lab."

"Any other advice for this over-worked and confused public servant?"

"Listen to your gut as well as your brain. You will need both to find the truth."

Hunter's dinner consisted of a Whopper and large order of onion rings from Burger King. As he walked into his house Graham knew it would be a long night. He was not going to sleep much until the killer was found. He put on Gustav Mahler's Requiem. Margo Elly deserved to be mourned with as much dignity as possible. Graham knew so little about the victim that he could not compose an appropriate eulogy, but he promised the dead woman that he would work tirelessly to bring her killer to justice. Then he raised a glass of his most expensive cabernet and asked for eternal peace for the deceased.

As the second movement of the symphony began, Graham poured himself another glass of wine and summoned two empiricists from the past, John Locke and David Hume, for help in the investigation. It was nearly impossible for a detective to adopt the philosophical tenets of the rationalists. The rationalists were not interested in particulars like the characteristics of a specific crime. They wanted to discover universal truths that applied to all crimes. Hunter and all detectives cared much less about universal truths. They needed to understand the particulars. Like all empiricists Hunter would begin this investigation with no preconceived ideas about the victim or the killer. He would only look at facts. Sensory data were not perfect, but they could be trusted a lot more than the ideas of most informants. Unfortunately, all forensic data (finger prints, blood, bodily fluids, tissue samples, fabric samples) had to be evaluated by fallible men, so some error was inevitable. The important thing for the investigator and the philosopher was to look for consensus: Did all of the separate pieces of evidence lead to the same conclusion? If not, the investigator had to find some way to explain the lack of consistency. The biggest problem for both philosophers and detectives was the human observer. Regrettably, many criminal investigations only had eye witness testimony to link the accused to the crime scene. Considerable research had shown that eye witnesses were unreliable observers. Rarely were they primed ahead of time to be data recorders; they simply had the bad luck to be in the vicinity of the crime when it happened. In addition, eye witnesses often had ulterior motives in giving their testimony. They might have a vendetta against the suspect, or they might want to hide their own involvement in the crime. Graham hoped that the forensic evidence would be abundant, so that he would not have to rely heavily on eye witness testimony to sort fact from fiction. Although his review of basic epistemology provided no concrete direction for the investigation, it provided a framework that hopefully would help the detective look at the evidence more objectively.

CHAPTER 19:
GRAHAM HUNTER OCTOBER 9

Hunter was enjoying his second cup of coffee and third donut when Kevin O' Rourke knocked on his door.

"Graham, none of Elly's neighbors heard or saw anything. The first responders also had no additional information. What did you learn?"

Hunter recounted his tour of the Elly's house, including the separate and disparate living quarters as well as the S & M room, and his conversation with Father Dominic.

"Graham, I almost forgot. The t-shirt that Margo Elly was wearing was the same one worn by the demonstrators against George Savage and the Program in Male Studies. It simply read 'STOP PMS NOW.'"

"Saul Alinsky, the famous community organizer, would like that. He always said that you must add humor to protests to keep the people going. Do you know of any connection between Margo Elly and the demonstrators?"

"Not really. She was a member of the Women's Studies Program, but she wasn't one of the leaders. She was much more involved in her research in biochemistry than promoting the feminist agenda."

"Nevertheless, the t-shirt indicates that she was clearly sympathetic to the campus feminists, and we already know that Elly had an ongoing battle with Savage."

"So, how do you want to proceed?"

"I want to interview Dr. Elly's research assistant and see what else I can learn about the victim. Then I will worry about Spearman and Savage. I would like you to return to the university and continue your inquiries about Primal Man. Any progress yet?"

"Not really. I have talked to nearly all of Savage's disciples. No one seems to have a clue regarding Primal Man's identity. They all swear that they would beat him to a pulp if they catch him."

"Keep probing. I want to get this guy off the street as soon as possible."

Hunter easily found the Euclidean Science Building. Finding Margo Elly's lab was a greater challenge. It was tucked away in the corner of a poorly lit basement—not a very prestigious location for a scientist who had a patent, thought Hunter. Was sexual discrimination rampant at the university, or was this slight directed at Margo Elly personally? Hunter stepped into the lab and was greeted by Elly's head research assistant. After identifying himself and offering his condolences, Hunter began his interrogation.

"Ms. Lacky, let me start with the obvious question: Can you think of anyone who might want to harm Dr. Elly?"

"Not really. Dr. Elly never talked about her personal life with me. We only talked about biochemistry."

"In the past few weeks did Dr. Elly seem upset or anxious about anything?"

"Ever since Emily Smith, one of her former research assistants, moved in with Dr. Savage she had been quite irritated. Dr. Elly never said anything to me, but I know she was both hurt and angry. Emily had been one of her prized pupils."

"Did Dr. Elly and Ms. Smith exchange any threats or harsh words?"

"I never witnessed any, but Emily told me that Dr. Elly scolded her for 'being foolish and acting like a bitch in heat.'"

"How did Emily respond?"

"She was hurt but not surprised. None of us had a personal relationship with Dr. Elly. We were just cogs in her research enterprise. Don't get me wrong; working with Dr. Elly helped all of us immensely in our careers, but she just wasn't someone you could get close to."

"Was there anything else unusual about Dr. Elly's behavior in the past few weeks?"

"Yes, she was preoccupied and detached which was atypical of her. In our morning meetings she didn't always track what the research assistants were saying. Finally, she stopped coming to the lab entirely."

"Any idea about what was bothering her besides Professor Savage?"

"It's just a guess, but I think she was extremely disappointed by the small attendance at the press conference announcing the establishment of her Young Women in Science Fund. Dr. Elly was so bummed-out that she forgot her speech. When the conference was over she went directly to her office, shut the door, and stayed there until the end of the day. It may be a coincidence, but her lapses in concentration started immediately after that."

"Finally, Ms. Lacky, do you know if Dr. Elly was romantically involved with anyone—any gossip or your own suspicions?"

A nervous laugh escaped from Judy Lacky. "Sorry, detective. If Dr. Elly was having an affair, none of us knew about it. I would be shocked to learn that she had a secret lover."

"Before I go would you mind showing me around?"

"Each of the four lab assistants has an office in a corner of the lab. This is our private space for writing and doing data analyses. The experiments themselves take place at one of the benches in the large common space in the middle of the lab. Dr. Elly's personal office is right down the hall. I have a key, if you want to see it."

"Yes, I would."

Judy Lacky unlocked the door for Hunter and returned to the lab. Margo Elly's office contained none of the clutter that was typically found in the offices of most university professors. Like her home everything in her office was meticulously organized. Journals were arranged alphabetically and by date of publication. Books were alphabetized within topic. Unlike the typical faculty member's desk which is layered with stacks of papers, books, and computer print-outs, Margo Elly's desk contained only a tape dispenser, a stapler, and a computer. No family pictures or artwork decorated her office walls. Two file cabinets contained class notes, reprints, computer out-put, and other files. Taped on every drawer was a list of its contents. Hunter opened the drawer labeled "University Business." His eyes were immediately drawn to two files labeled "Savage" and "Spearman." In each folder was a single sheet of paper entitled "victims" which listed the names of women and phone numbers. Graham quickly copied the information. Surprisingly Margo Elly's computer was turned on and her email folder was open. Hunter couldn't resist. He would worry about a search warrant later. Only ten messages were in the IN file. Most of them concerned university business, but Hunter's eyes were immediately attracted to three emails, one from Spearman, a second from Savage, and a third from Primal Man. All three of them threatened Margo Elly with bodily harm. Hurriedly, he printed the three messages and put them in his pocket. The SENT file only contained eight emails and none were directed to the suspects. The DELETE file was empty. Margo Elly's email habits were consistent with the rest of her life—organized and pristine, but not very revealing.

Hunter locked the door and returned the key to Judy Lacky. "Ms. Lacky, did anyone besides Dr. Elly have access to her computer?"

"The janitors, the campus police, and I all have keys to her office. However, to use the computer you would need to know Dr. Elly's password. I don't think she would have shared that with anyone."

"That's odd. When I searched her office, her file drawers were unlocked and her computer was on. Ms. Lacky, you're a scientist. Any hypotheses?"

"Well, as I told you, she was still very upset about the poor attendance at the press conference and Emily. Maybe she was just so preoccupied and distracted that she forgot to turn off the computer and lock the file cabinets."

"Thanks, Ms. Lacky. Here is my card. Please call me if you think of anything else."

Hunter drove immediately to the county prosecutor's office. He needed a search warrant in order to legally seize the computer and other evidence. It would hardly be wise for him to have a frank and open conversation with Justin Mather on this topic. Fortunately, the county prosecutor accepted Graham's rather vague articulation of the necessity of searching Margo Elly's office.

"Graham, this may be the first time that we were in agreement," said Mather sarcastically. "Dr. Elly's office should be searched. Perhaps we'll find a threatening message from our little pervert."

"Justin, you have to get over your fixation with Primal Man," responded an exasperated Hunter. "Primal Man is hardly our only suspect; Dr. Elly had a lot of enemies."

"Stop protecting the little faggot, Graham. Trust me. These queers harbor so much hate for our societal values that it takes very little for them to explode"

"No offense, Justin, but we found no evidence of forced entry. It's hard to believe that Dr. Elly would have admitted someone to her home who was wearing a ski mask and black vinyl raincoat."

"Perhaps the little prick wasn't wearing his costume on the night he struck down Dr. Elly."

"Enough! I don't have time to debate this with you now. Let's get the search warrant."

With little discussion Judge Solomon signed the document. In less than an hour Hunter was in Chief Gunn's office serving the warrant. Gunn made a mild protest and called the university's legal department. By the end of the day Hunter had legally obtained the same evidence that he had surreptitiously acquired earlier. He also took a copy of Margo Elly's curriculum vitae, hoping that it would provide some information about her death as well as her life.

CHAPTER 20:
FATHER DOMINIC OCTOBER 9

Father Dominic meandered aimlessly through the campus. He felt angry and helpless. He had grown to love everything about Dephi University—the physical space, the students, the faculty, and even most of the administrators. Now the university was adrift. The campus vacillated between anarchy and lethargy. The quadrangle was virtually deserted these days. Before Primal Man made his first appearance hundreds of students gathered in this bucolic space and enjoyed the beauty that surrounded them. The lawn would be covered with students. Some engaged in solitary reading; others threw Frisbees. Couples caressed and pecked at each other, while faculty and staff took positions on the benches and spied on the young lovers wistfully. Witnessing the energy and carefree manner of the students made the older generation feel younger and more vigorous. Large oak trees, maples, and red sumac framed this pastoral setting. Today only a few students observed and enjoyed the display of color provided by fall's foliage. Nature's canvas of brilliant yellows, deep oranges, fiery crimson, and burgundy didn't exist for the vast majority of the Delphi students and faculty. The campus now had two hundred fewer female students. Primal Man and Margo Elly's killer had chased them home. The spontaneity and energy of the remaining women had been drained dry. Few of them ventured out after dark. Fraternity and sorority parties had disappeared. Even during daylight few women could be found walking around campus alone. They sought protection from a boyfriend or a cadre of female friends.

The majority of Delphi males had become immobile in thought and deed. They detested both the radical feminists and the PMS program. Their traditional ways of interacting with their female compatriots were no longer appreciated or effective. These unfortunate men were clueless about how to support the women that shared their classrooms, offices, and beds. Horny and helpless they medicated themselves with sports and alcohol.

Most of the faculty detested the PMS program and the actions of Hilda German and her allies, but their strong belief in academic freedom made it difficult for them to take action under the auspices of the Faculty Senate. Teachers continued to hold classes, but all of the intellectual energy had been sucked from the university community. Dom was at a loss for what to do. Helping Hunter search for Primal Man and Margo Elly's killer didn't seem enough. He had prayed for guidance, but his God was silent.

CHAPTER 21:
HILDA GERMAN OCTOBER 10

Margo Elly's death had only fueled Hilda German's war against everyone associated with the PMS. She was convinced that Primal Man, George Savage, or some other chauvinist had murdered Margo Elly. She was even more incensed that President Sinduce had refused her demand to eliminate the Program in Male Studies. Hilda had pleaded, "Doesn't murder trump academic freedom, Madame President?"

Sinduce had simply shrugged her shoulders and said, "Dr. German, I cannot overturn the decisions of the curriculum committee." Then the president tried to bribe her with an offer of a sabbatical to England for a year.

German had concluded the meeting with a threat, "If you will not protect the women of this university, I will."

Twenty-two hours after storming out of Sinduce's office Hilda German held a press conference. Over five hundred people were jammed into the auditorium waiting for her arrival. Reporters from CNN, FOX, and other national media outlets competed with Maria Flores and other local reporters for space close to the podium. The audience sensed that some unknown, but fantastic, spectacle was going to take place. Uniformed campus police stood guard at the foot of the stage and patrolled the aisles. City police had been deputized to monitor the exits of the auditorium and remainder of the campus.

German delayed her appearance until she could feel the floor vibrate from the crowd noise. She was dressed in military fatigues with black armbands in memory of Margo Elly. A black beret covered her head. On her left front pocket was a red badge that displayed a closed fist raised in the salute made famous by the Black Panthers. Her young supporters, the New Amazons, were also dressed in combat fatigues, waving their "STOP PMS NOW" signs furiously. Their angry mantra, "Savage! Savage! You're a knave. You and Primal Man belong in a cave," echoed throughout the auditorium. Darwin's Disciples, the name chosen by Savage's followers, tried to compete with the New Amazons, but they were hopelessly outnumbered. Their refrain of "German! German! You're no fun. Your New Amazons had better run," was only audible to themselves. Once again the young feminists resumed their chant and stomped their feet. German waited a good ten minutes before she motioned for her army to sit down.

"My dear sisters," she began, "Male chauvinists have once again slain one of our own. Just a few days ago Professor Margo Elly was brutally murdered in her own home. Today her killer and Primal Man's descendants remain free to wage their assault on women everywhere. We must band together, or we will never eliminate the male scum that plague us daily. Today, my sisters, I declare war on the Program in Male Studies and its supporters, including Primal Man. The women of this campus will no longer passively stand by and watch our gender be insulted by the intellectually dishonest and morally bankrupt ideas of George Savage and his fellow sociobiologists. Both the academy and the larger society must rid themselves of this menace. I urge all of you to join me in fighting this war. If our campus administration will not eliminate the PMS, then we must take matters into our own hands. We refuse to allow the purveyors of falsehood to continue to spread their misogynist gospel with impunity. Therefore, truth squads will constantly shadow every faculty member who teaches in the Program of Male Studies. We will not permit them to promulgate their lies under the guise of academic freedom. They will be silenced! We need volunteers to sign on as guerillas to disrupt every PMS class. We will also provide armed escorts for any sister who fears for her safety. In addition, we will begin patrolling the campus, scouting for suspicious characters and activities. Members of our army, the New Amazons, are now circulating throughout the auditorium ready to enlist you in this war. Please join us. Take no prisoners, my sisters."

German concluded her speech with a raised fist that was the signal for her supporters to resume stomping their feet and screaming their now familiar hymn. Maria Flores and other reporters shouted questions at General German, but she ignored them, exited stage left, and was escorted to her office by six large supporters. The police prevented a confrontation between the New Amazons and Darwin's Disciples by forcefully escorting the smaller male contingent out of the auditorium immediately at the conclusion of German's speech. Today was a victory for Hilda German and her soldiers.

General German was on such an adrenaline rush when the spectacle of her call to arms ended that she could not return to the mundane routine of a university professor for the rest of the day. Confidently she walked from the campus and strolled through the Agora. The merchants proudly displayed their Greek heritage in both their dress and the décor of their stores. Hilda loved looking at the carpets, jewelry, and replicas of classical pottery. The grocery store and the bakery were Hilda's favorite places in the Agora. The food was authentic and delicious. Craving sugar she purchased two slices of baklava and continued strolling through the market place. A small child dressed in the traditional tunic tugged at her arm as she savored the last bit of the honey laden dessert. The usually serious Hilda German smiled at the little waif who tugged at her shirt and offered to escort her to the Temple of the Oracle. She placed a dollar in her guide's small hand and entered the ante room. German thought that the peplos of the priestess was too provacative, but she still found a sense of peace in the temple. As she entered the sanctuary the smell of burning leaves rose from the grates. A sympathetic voice inquired,

"What counsel do you seek from the Oracle, my sister?"

"How can I make my colleagues understand the dangers of the PMS program?"

"You must use the fire that burns within you to illuminate the darkness."

Puzzled, but somehow reassured, German exited the temple and made her way home. A glass of Riesling completed her spiritual and physical renewal.

CHAPTER 22:
GRAHAM HUNTER OCTOBER 11

O'Rourke was waiting for Hunter when he arrived at work the next day.

"Graham, you won't believe this. Savage has been exiled to Africa. The university gave him a paid leave to pursue his research. His graduate assistant is now teaching the class."

"Typical corporate response to trouble makers—bribe them to leave town and keep quiet. The administration is hoping that Hilda German and the others will stop the demonstrations if Savage is out of the picture, but they underestimate these women. They won't stop until the Program in Male Studies is dismantled."

"German has already increased the heat. She organized a huge rally against Savage and the PMS. She calls her young supporters, the New Amazons. German and her army dress in military fatigues, and they have a lot of angry energy. It's pretty scary."

"I was afraid something like this might happen. You and O'Malley need to monitor the movements of this new army and keep me informed."

"Graham, how do you think Primal Man will respond to Savage's scheduled departure and German's declaration of war?"

"Two competing hypotheses: (1) Primal Man's courage and cock shrivel up and he disappears forever; or (2) Primal Man decides to avenge Savage and becomes more confrontational."

"I don't think Primal Man is going away."

"Then we need to catch this guy soon."

"We are working every night, but so far Kathy has been unable to entice our flasher."

"Don't give up. One of these days he won't be able to resist the challenge."

"Any developments in the Elly case, Graham?"

Hunter recounted his interview with Judy Lacky, particularly the information about the affair between Savage and Emily Smith. Then he handed O'Rourke copies of the email messages and asked him to read each one aloud and comment.

O'Rourke read, "'Stop harassing Dr. Savage, or Primal Man will take his revenge.' This doesn't make sense. German, not Elly, was behind the demonstrations against Savage."

"Don't forget, Elly was angry at Savage for seducing her favorite research assistant."

"True, but that assumes that Primal Man knew about Elly's dispute with Savage—not likely."

"How about Savage's message?"

Kevin read, "'Elly, leave me alone, or you will regret it. I'll fuck whomever I please, including Emily Smith.' This message seems consistent with your description of Savage's personality (egotistical, hotheaded, and impulsive)."

"And the email from Spearman?"

"'Ice Queen, it's time for my revenge.' Sorry, Graham, I don't know enough about Spearman to hazard a guess."

"Kevin, does it seem strange to you that Elly received three threatening emails from three suspects one week prior to her murder?"

"Perhaps there were earlier messages, but she deleted them. You said she was a neat freak."

"Can we find out if there were other emails?"

"I think so. Most large organizations have back-up systems that retain this information for several years. I will check with the university computer center."

"If they balk at your request, tell them we will hold a press conference detailing their lack of cooperation in a murder investigation. I will arrange for the FBI computer geeks to analyze what you find. We don't have that expertise in the Delphi police department."

After Kevin left his office, Graham called Maria Flores and arranged to have dinner with her that night. He didn't give her the details about Savage's African exile. He suspected that she would be outraged and disheartened to learn that he had once again escaped punishment for his sordid behavior. Somehow he wanted to comfort and protect her. As he hung up the phone Graham realized that he was whipped. It wasn't just lust that he was experiencing, but the whole gamut of emotions associated with being in love.

As planned Graham arrived at Maria's apartment at eight with Chinese food. Maria was wearing a purple v-neck sweater. On several occasions Graham had to resort to the beet trick after his gaze had drifted toward Maria's cleavage. He hoped that she had not noticed his lechery. After the pot stickers and hot and sour soup, Graham spoke, "Maria, I have good news, and I have bad news."

"Okay, I am ready. The Merlot will fortify me."

"Savage is going to Africa."

"You're kidding! Is that the good news, or the bad news?"

"Both. I'm happy for the women of Delphi University, but I think his departure may put a damper on your exclusive."

"Not necessarily. There obviously is a story behind his sudden disappearance."

"I think the story is a simple one. The university administration wants the demonstrations stopped. They bribed him with a paid leave to pursue his research."

"What cowards!"

"Agreed! Sinduce et al. are hoping that Hilda German will not be able to rally her troops without Savage as a target. I believe that the university administration has underestimated the dedication of Dr. German and the New Amazons."

"How will Savage's departure affect your investigation of Primal Man and the Elly murder?"

"I don't know if Savage's disgrace will deflate Primal Man or anger him to do something more violent. I feel more worried than hopeful, however."

"That scares me, Graham. I usually find more truth in feelings than thoughts"

Graham instinctively reached across the table for Maria's hand, and tried to reassure her with his eyes. Then a frustrated look came across his face. "Sorry, Maria. My beeper just went off. Can I use your phone?"

"It's in the bedroom."

Upon entering the room Graham temporarily forgot his page; his senses were overwhelmed by the presence of Maria Flores. The scents coming from her perfume bottles and the basket of potpourri excited him as did the sight of her lingerie draped over a chair. On her nightstand were several books in Spanish. On her dresser were pictures of people of all ages—her family he presumed. Most of the photos captured scenes of a large family enjoying each other—children playing at the beach, a family dinner, a wedding celebration. A photo of a distinguished older couple in riding clothes seemed to watch over the other photos.

Graham regained his focus and made his call. Primal Man had struck again.

"Maria, I'm sorry. I have to go to the station. There has been another flashing incident."

"Was the victim hurt?"

"Not physically."

Kathy O'Malley was waiting for Hunter when he arrived at the station. "Kathy, good to see you again. Can you fill me in?"

"Pretty much the same modus operandi (vinyl raincoat, ski mask, orange condom). However, this time Primal Man chose a particular target for his assault. The victim was wearing the uniform of the New Amazons, and the message was quite specific."

Graham read the note aloud, "Bitch, your army of lesbians is no match for Primal Man. Stop harassing the PMS, or Margo Elly will not be the only one to die."

Graham gave Kathy O'Malley a worried look. "How's the victim?"

"I think she'll be okay. She is more angry than anxious; that's a good sign."

"Was she able to give you any new information about Primal Man?"

"Yes. The victim called the flasher a pathetic pervert when he opened his raincoat. The perpetrator responded by opening his mouth as if to speak, but he couldn't. Angrily he flung his message at the victim and sprinted toward the woods."

"Now we know why Primal Man always delivers his messages on index cards. He has some kind of speech impediment. Anything else, Kathy?"

"No, sir."

After O'Malley left, Graham methodically reread the file on Primal Man hoping to find a clue that he had overlooked, but no new insights emerged. Trying to channel the nervous energy that possessed him, Graham rapidly paced around his desk. Then he grabbed his tennis ball and once again began the holy ceremony by repeatedly bouncing the ball off the wall, but the ritual failed him. Totally discouraged he tossed the tennis ball into his desk drawer, closed the file, and slowly ambled toward the Agora. He needed advice. A little pixie dressed in tunic, sandals, and an imitation laurel wreath tugged at his sleeve and led him to the temple. Graham slipped some coins into the child's hand and greeted the priestess warmly. She returned his smile demurely and led him to the sanctuary. Once again the aroma of incense rose from the floor grates. A strong authoritative voice greeted him.

"Seeker of truth and justice, how can I help you?"

"Is Primal Man dangerous?"

"Sound and fury follow him everywhere."

The prophecy only confirmed Graham's worst fears, but oddly he felt reassured. Somehow he would unmask Primal Man. He bid farewell to the priestess and strolled down the street. As he walked through the door of his home he wondered what his mother would have thought of his visit to a pagan temple. She probably would have insisted that he receive the sacrament of penance for violating the first commandment.

CHAPTER 23:
PRIMAL MAN OCTOBER 11

After a brief sprint through the woods Primal Man found a safe place to stop and change from his battle gear to his regular clothes. He stowed his uniform in his backpack, took a deep breath, and calmly made his way to his dorm. Inside the safety of his room he reflected upon the events of the last two days. He hated to admit it, but Darwin's Disciples had embarrassed the entire PMS program with their weak performance at German's rally. They had acted like frightened little boys, not real men. Not only were they outnumbered by the New Amazons, but they lacked the discipline of the feminists. The New Amazons had uniforms, signs, a battle cry, and a lot of energy. They also had a charismatic leader. Professor German was a castrating bitch, but she sure could give a speech. None of the PMS faculty, including Professor Savage, seemed willing to organize an army to fight this assault on their biological rights and duties as men.

Primal Man hoped that tonight's attack on one of German's soldiers would be enough to inspire the PMS faculty to organize a counter attack. He knew that he could not win this fight alone. He deeply regretted his inability to respond to the lesbo when she called him a pervert. Once again his vocal cords had failed him. She, and all of the radical feminists, needed to know that he was not a sexual deviant, but a man defending the natural rights of his gender.

Worn out from the day's activities he climbed into bed and began his nightly ritual of praying the rosary, but after one decade he threw his deceased grandmother's rosary at the wall. The chain broke and the sapphire colored beads scattered in every direction. He was angry at Jesus and the Virgin for not curing him of his speech stigmata. For twenty-one years he had been a good Catholic. He had prayed fervently that his speech impediment would be eradicated, but his prayers had gone unanswered. God had abandoned him. Tearfully he slumped to the floor and began collecting the sapphire beads and carefully placed them along with the crucifix and silver chain in the small leather pouch used to carry the rosary. He hoped that his grandmother would forgive him.

CHAPTER 24:
DONALD SPEAK OCTOBER 12

Donald Speak, the usually gregarious Director of University Communications, had suddenly become an introvert after the Elly murder. Not only were Maria Flores and other local reporters hounding him, but the national media were pursuing him like a pack of howling dogs on a fox hunt. The ferocity and volume of their barking kept increasing every day. Nothing that Speak said satisfied their hunger for more red meat. Even CNN had sent a crew to cover the story. Speak feared that the media would link Margo Elly's murder with the conflict between the New Amazon's and Darwin's Disciples. If that connection were made, panic would seize the entire Delphi community. Speak had begged the police department to issue a statement indicating that Dr. Elly's murder was not related to the flashing incidents and campus demonstrations. Detective Hunter had refused, saying that such a statement was premature.

Anxious and depressed Speak gulped his third scotch of the evening. Without the numbing effects of alcohol he could not fall asleep these days. He was sixty-two years old, balding, overweight, and wore thick glasses. The broken veins in his face and nose indicated that drinking had been his coping mechanism for many years. Prior to arriving at Delphi University some twenty years ago he had been in advertising. The pressure of coming up with clever slogans and eye-catching graphic designs had been too much for him. Delphi University had been an ideal place for the extroverted, but stress-avoidant, Speak to work. It was a quiet liberal arts school where working class parents who feared the anonymity and immorality of large state universities sent their children to be educated. Neither the faculty nor President Sinduce made many demands on him. Twice a week or so he would craft press releases regarding curriculum changes or the exploits of one of the athletic teams known as the Delphi Spartans. Occasionally, he had to organize a press conference for President Sinduce or a faculty member who had published a book. The rest of the time he spent in his office reading or watching TV.

Recent events, however, had destroyed his relaxed way of life. His chummy relationship with the press no longer existed. Reporters were constantly demanding more information about Primal Man, the gender war, and the Elly murder. They accused the communications director and his superiors of a cover-up and complicity in the crime wave that had swept the campus. Hilda German had made things even worse by holding her own press conference and threatening to close down the campus.

Speak also worried about the mental health of his colleague and close friend, Liz Gold. Even before Primal Man had started exposing himself to Delphi co-eds she had raised little money for the MOM. Gold had initially approached her job in a very professional manner, making calls at places of business, dressing in suits with blouses buttoned at the neck, and wearing little make-up. In recent months, however, she had been meeting prospects in bars. She wore push-up bras and cocktail dresses that displayed significant cleavage. Her lips, nails, and eye lids were painted in bright colors that made her look more like a prostitute than a university development officer. This degrading approach to raising money had led to many propositions, but no new gifts to the university. Speak feared that his friend had little chance of success regardless of what tactics she employed to snare a prospective donor. The major industries in this section of Missouri were lead mining and timber. The owners of these enterprises occasionally contributed money to the School of Business or the College of Engineering, but Speak doubted that they would give a dime for the MOM.

CHAPTER 25:
GRAHAM HUNTER OcTOBER 14

Hunter began his day with another sugary breakfast of pastry from Alongi's bakery and several cups of coffee. Two envelopes on his desk begged to be opened. One contained the official autopsy report in medical jargon. The other envelope contained the "Cliff Notes" version. For years the medical examiner had been providing Graham this courtesy in exchange for a bottle of red wine, preferably pinot noir. The condensed version of the report read as follows:

> Time of death is estimated between 10 pm on October 6 and 5 am on October 7. Examination of the body of the victim revealed no evidence of severe trauma to the head, abdomen, or other part of the body that could have caused death. Also no fractures were found. The small fang-like cuts found on each breast may have been inflicted by a staple remover. The cuts caused only minor bleeding. Bruises were found on the inner thighs, buttocks, and hamstring muscles. None of these injuries were severe enough to have caused death, individually or cumulatively. All of the bruises could have been caused by the miniature bat that was found lying near the victim. However, many other objects could have caused similar marks. There was no bruising on the wrists caused by the manacles, suggesting that the victim did not resist being handcuffed.
>
> The victim's entire body and clothing were examined carefully for DNA evidence. Head, vagina, mouth, and finger nails were given special attention. Only the victim's DNA was found. No finger prints were found on the baseball bat or anywhere else. No semen

was found. Inspection of the contents of the victim's stomach and other tissues found no evidence of drugs or poison. She had, however, had several glasses of wine.

Examination of the victim's heart indicated that she probably died because of a myocardial infarction. It is possible that the victim may have experienced a drastic increase in the amount of epinephrine in her body as a result of the stress of the assault which could have triggered a cardiac arrhythmia that led to the myocardial infarction. The body's natural response to stress is to release epinephrine to assist with the flight-fight response. Excessive amounts of epinephrine will cause both blood pressure and heart rate to increase, possibly resulting in cardiac arrhythmia. Unfortunately, this conjecture cannot be proved, because the body releases massive amounts of epinephrine in the act of dying regardless of the cause of death. Nevertheless, I believe this explanation of the victim's death is the one most consistent with the evidence available to us. Finally, it should be noted that examination of the victim's medical records revealed no history of cardiac problems, including arrhythmias.

Much of the autopsy report mystified Hunter. Dr. Elly had not resisted her attacker. Lack of scratches on her wrists indicated that she had consented to being handcuffed, and there was no major trauma to her body. This did not appear to be a stranger rape. The lack of forced entry also suggested that Margo Elly probably knew her attacker. Hunter had two theories that were consistent with the majority of the evidence. In the "rape fantasy gone wrong" theory Elly was a consenting actress in the "rape drama," allowing her attacker to gag and handcuff her. Perhaps she even consented to the small cuts on her breasts. However, one important fact was difficult to reconcile with this theory? If Elly were a willing partner in this drama, why would she become scared to death? Hunter could only generate one hypothesis that explained how her sadomasochistic fantasy could suddenly turn into a deadly nightmare. Her leading man had stopped play-acting; for some reason he had changed the ending of the play. A simulated rape was not a sufficient climax for his drama; only death would satisfy him. Had Margo Elly refused to gratify his sexual fantasies in some way that precipitated his rage, or had the assailant planned her murder from the beginning?

The "rape as ruse" theory also assumed that Elly knew her attacker. The theory hypothesized that the murderer had intended to kill her from the outset, perhaps with some hard to detect chemical agent. However, because of his sadistic wish to watch the victim squirm and plead for her life, as well as his need to divert the police from the real cause of death, the killer staged a rape. The rape scenario was so convincing that he literally scared Margo Elly to death, making it unnecessary to poison her.

The lack of semen in any orifice was consistent with the "rape as ruse" theory. The perpetrator according to this explanation had never lusted for Margo Elly. The lack of semen was harder to explain with the "rape fantasy gone wrong" theory. However, it was possible that the perpetrator's lust literally shrunk when Elly rejected him; all that remained was a murderous rage that kept escalating. Hunter could only speculate on the specific technique that the murderer used to scare the victim to death. Did he hold a knife to her throat? Did he place a gun to her head, and slowly, methodically pull the trigger multiple times? The presence of a weapon, particularly a gun, might explain the lack of a struggle.

Hunter spent the rest of the day pondering which theory applied to each of his suspects. Mike Hammer was the only one that fit the rape fantasy scenario, but why would he rape his wife in the kitchen when the couple had their own special playroom? Hunter did not think that it was plausible for Elly to participate in a rape fantasy with a stranger like Primal Man or a known enemy like Spearman or Savage.

Hunter could picture both Savage and Spearman perpetrating the "rape as ruse" drama given their hate for Dr. Elly and their histories as sexual predators. However, if either of these sociopaths were planning this murder, why would they throw suspicion on themselves by sending threatening emails? Was their impulse control that weak? Primal Man's most recent messages, including his email to Margo Elly, clearly indicated that the flasher was getting more agitated. Hunter could not imagine Dr. Elly admitting anyone to her home masked and wearing a black vinyl raincoat. However, could Primal Man have gained entry to the victim's home, if he had not been wearing his costume? Hunter hated to entertain any hypothesis of his nemesis, Justin Mather, but Primal Man could not be eliminated as a suspect.

Graham arrived home with a dinner of a meat lover's pizza from Pizza Hut. A refreshing heifivisen from Schafley's Brewery was probably too good a beer for the mediocre pizza. Tonight Graham chose Bob Dylan as his musical companion. The man was a genius in creating the lyrics of protest songs. As he relaxed in his favorite recliner he reviewed his approach to the investigation. He feared that he had abandoned empiricism and had been corrupted by rationalism and had generated theories of the crime too early in the investigation. He wanted to act like a scientist. He convinced himself that he had used the inductive method to create two plausible explanations for the crime. Now he had to rely on deductive methods to test the validity of the two theories. Tests designed to falsify competing conjectures was the next step in the scientific method according to Karl Popper, but in reality most scientists designed experiments to verify their hypotheses rather than challenge their validity. Graham aspired to approach the problem as Popper would, but he knew that he was looking harder for evidence to convict one suspect rather than seeking evidence to exonerate all suspects. Oh well, reason need not always be pure!

CHAPTER 26:
MARIA FLORES OCTOBER 14

Maria Flores had not seen Hunter in three days. Despite her intellectual resolve not to get involved with the Yanquee cop, her hormones were leading her in the opposite direction. She hated to admit it, but she missed the shy gringo. She worried that he was avoiding her. She could not decide if his evasion was personal or professional. Was he afraid of becoming involved with any woman, or had he never really been interested in her? She tried to reassure herself that his lack of contact must be due to the time he was spending searching for Primal Man and Elly's killer.

Against her will Maria had devoted hours analyzing her feelings for Hunter. Although he was moderately handsome, his values and character were his special attraction. He truly cared about people, particularly anyone who had been a victim of a crime. He sincerely believed that the police and the courts were instruments of justice. Based on her experience in Chile, Maria had a hard time accepting this concept. Nevertheless, she admired his faith in the system. She definitely wanted to help him capture Primal Man and Elly's murderer. Did she want to be his soul mate as well? Once again she begged the Virgin Mother to stifle her feelings for the cop with the indigo eyes. However, she knew that her prayer would go unanswered once again.

BOOK 3

SIFTING THROUGH THE EVIDENCE

If a man will begin with certainties, he shall end in doubts: but if he will be content to begin with doubts, he shall end in certainties.(Francis Bacon)

Experience without theory is blind, but theory without experience is mere intellectual play. (Immanuel Kant)

CHAPTER 27:
DONALD SPEAK OCTOBER 15

Normally Donald Speak dreaded President Sinduce's cabinet meetings; they were as dull as a treatise on logical positivism by A. J. Ayer. Today was different; the president announced that she was creating a new position, Vice President (VP) for Innovative Technology (IT). She explained that the new VP would create partnerships between Delphi University and local industries that would result in patents and new research opportunities for faculty and students.

"Patents," emphasized Sinduce, "will produce revenue for the Museum of Medicine. Our development director obviously needs help in raising money." Sinduce paused and looked directly at Liz Gold who hardly looked professional with her slip showing and a run in her fish net stockings.

Speak broke the silence, "Excellent idea, Madame President. Whom shall we put on the search committee?"

"There will be no search, Donald. I have already selected the man for the position."

With that announcement the doors to the cabinet room were thrust open and in strutted Delphi's first VP of IT. He was obviously a man who wanted to be noticed. He wore an Armani double-breasted black suit, pearl gray shirt, scarlet tie and matching handkerchief. His shoes were Italian and his watch a Rolex. His thick wavy hair was black as coal and heavily moussed. Depending on your perspective his eye movements could be described as mysterious, mischievous, or shifty, but never innocent or naive.

The new VP took the vacant seat at the end of the long walnut conference table, directly facing President Sinduce. "Let me introduce Owen Nigel Onan, our new Vice President for Innovative Technology," pronounced the president.

After the polite applause and forced smiles of the other cabinet members had ceased, Onan addressed the assembly. "Let me be blunt. This university is in the Dark Ages with regard to maximizing its revenue possibilities. I guarantee that within one year we will be breaking ground on a new research park that will house companies that are at the cutting edge of both biomedical research and information technology. Within five years this campus will reap annual revenue of more than five million dollars from patents generated by those enterprises. If the current faculty is unable or unwilling to participate in this venture, we will hire new faculty who wish to be part of the 21st century instead of worshipers of the past. Currently only the late Dr. Elly has secured a patent, and for some mysterious reason University Communications has not successfully promoted her discovery. What could be more interesting to the public than a new contraceptive? Mr. Speak, you will have to do better in the future. Now, if you will excuse me, I must oversee the renovation of my office."

A few minutes later President Sinduce adjourned the meeting. She asked Speak to remain behind for a chat. "So, Donald, what do you think of Mr. Onan?"

"I am not sure, Bertha. I like the idea of the new position, but what do we know about him? Quite frankly he strikes me as an arrogant self-promoter."

"Perhaps, Donald, but what can I do? Liz has been a failure as our development director. I need someone to raise the money for the MOM."

With that exchange the conversation ended. As Speak left the room Sinduce pivoted her chair and stared at the Elysian Fields. Speak suspected that she did not see the prairie grass blowing in the wind or the wild flowers enjoying the last bit of Indian summer. She only saw a vision of the MOM standing tall. Speak bowed his head and left the president's office. He needed a drink to escape his predicament.

CHAPTER 28:
MARIA FLORES OCTOBER 16

A memorial service for Margo Elly was held at the non-denominational chapel at Delphi University, because the deceased had no religious affiliation. Maria Flores stationed herself in one of the back pews in order to observe all the mourners. Less than thirty people were in attendance. Mike Hammer sat alone in the first pew on the right. He looked extremely uncomfortable in his out of style Edwardian suit which was two sizes too small. The top button of his faded white shirt was unbuttoned, probably a relic from an era when he was less rotund. His wide paisley tie was vintage early seventies as were his shoes with their square toes and buckles. Two professional looking males sat a few rows back from Hammer—colleagues from the biochemistry department presumed Maria. The press made up the rest of the delegation on the right.

Hilda German sat in the first pew on the left. Behind her sat three middle aged women who were probably faculty in the Women's Study Program. Further back sat two younger women; Maria surmised that they were Elly's lab assistants. Another young woman dressed in business attire sat alone in the next to last row. Maria wasn't sure where she fit in the puzzle. Hunter entered the small chapel just as the service was beginning and sat in the pew immediately opposite Maria. She flashed him a clandestine wink.

The service lasted less than twenty minutes. The university chaplain made a brief invocation and asked the Lord to forgive Margo Elly for her sins and welcome her into his kingdom. Hilda German praised Dr. Elly for her contributions to the Women's Studies Program, but she provided few specifics. The lack of tears or any affect made it clear to Maria that Hilda German was not grieving for the deceased.

Owen Nigel Onan, the new VP of IT, made the closing speech. His ensemble was too "Madison Avenue" and his grooming too manicured to be an academic. Maria quickly labeled Onan as a self-absorbed egotist who had more interest in being noticed than pursuing truth or wisdom. The eulogy was carefully crafted. Onan cited Elly's devotion to science and the importance of her patent in revolutionizing family planning around the world. He then concluded, "But her greatest passion was for young women scientists. As most of you know Dr. Elly established the Women in Science Fund to provide scholarships for promising women scientists. You can remember her and support her vision by contributing to her fund. For your convenience envelopes addressed to the Innovative Technology office have been placed in all of the pews."

After Onan's crass appeal for donations the funeral service abruptly ended with no concluding prayer or recessional music. Pretty sad to be mourned in this manner, thought Maria. Only in the eyes of Mike Hammer did the journalist see any tears.

Onan's financial hustling at this somber event had physically upset Maria. Simultaneously, she felt like vomiting and kicking Onan in the groin. The absence of any family members at the service also made a big impression on her. The journalist, however, was more curious about the professionally dressed woman who sat alone. The mystery woman left immediately after the service. Maria followed her to the parking lot. "Excuse me, miss. I am Maria Flores, reporter for the Scribe."

The woman froze, panic stricken. Maria presented her business card. "I'm sorry that I startled you. I am working on a feature article on the work of Dr. Elly. I have been interviewing people who knew her in hopes of finding out more about both her professional and personal life. Would you mind talking to me for a few minutes?"

"Oh, uh . . . , sure, if it won't take long. I have to get back to work soon."

"No problem. If we are unable to finish the interview, I can call you later. Do you have a business card?"

"Dr. Melissa Hope, biochemist, Frazier Pharmaceuticals," read Maria. "Dr. Hope, may I ask your connection with Dr. Elly?"

"She was my doctoral advisor, but I haven't seen her since she hooded me two years ago. I probably haven't talked to her in a year."

"No other contact since then?"

"No, my professional work has gone in a different direction, and I was not personally close to Dr. Elly."

"Pardon my inquisitiveness, but it strikes me as unusual that you would attend the funeral of someone you were not close to professionally or personally."

"Me too when I think about it. Dr. Elly was not a lovable woman. She was demanding; she frequently criticized your work and challenged your commitment to science. She never uttered one word of praise for good work; she just expected it. I can't explain my presence here today; it was some type of compulsion."

"Let me switch topics. Do you know anything about Dr. Elly's family?"

"Sorry, no. She never talked about her family."

"Did you know her husband?"

"No. Was the fat guy in the front pew her husband?"

"Yes."

"Wow, it's hard to believe that Dr. Elly would be married to someone—how should I say it—that was not impeccably groomed. Her clothes were always perfect, and she never had a hair out of place. Quite a contrast! Sorry, that was not very charitable."

"That's okay. Is there anything else that you can think of that might be relevant to my article?"

"No, not really."

"Thanks for your help. Feel free to call me if you remember anything about Dr. Elly regardless of how inconsequential it seems."

Maria walked slowly back to her car. She was puzzled. Melissa Hope's description of Margo Elly was consistent with the views of other members of the university community, namely that she was a cold, unfeeling tyrant. Why did she attend her funeral then? Simple curiosity was not a sufficient explanation for this journalist. Her analytical mind told her that Melissa Hope was more involved with Margo Elly than she had revealed so far.

CHAPTER 29:
GRAHAM HUNTER OCTOBER 17

When Graham arrived at his office Kevin O'Rourke was waiting for him. He had just finished another stake-out with O'Malley that had failed to arouse Primal Man. Nevertheless, he had a big smile on his face. "Graham, guess who was caught leaving Margo Elly's house?"

"Kevin, don't be so coy. Spill the beans."

"Mike Hammer. A patrolman arrested him as he was dragging a large trunk from the house."

"I think it is time for me to read Mr. Hammer his rights. Do you want to join me?"

"I wish I could, but I have to go to class. Make sure you take good notes on the sex stuff; I could use some new techniques."

Graham smiled. Kevin had certainly loosened up since they had first started working together on the campus flasher case. O'Rourke was a rare cop. He was dedicated and smart, but he wasn't consumed by the job. He would not become overwhelmed by the human misery, disturbing pathology, and pure evil that confronted homicide detectives. He would not let the sixty percent rate of unsolved cases overwhelm him.

Hunter walked over to the section of the police station which contained the holding cells and the interrogation rooms. Mike Hammer was seated in the room in handcuffs and ankle shackles. He was sweating profusely and looked extremely anxious.

"Sorry about the cuffs," Hunter began. "Oh, but I forgot. You like that sort of thing, don't you Mr. Hammer?"

Hammer said nothing. He simply bowed his head sheepishly.

"I understand that you have already been informed of your Miranda rights, so let me review where things stand now. We are definitely going to charge you with removing evidence from a crime scene. Murder is another possible charge, but I don't want to jump to conclusions."

"I didn't kill her. I told you she was already dead when I got home."

"You must admit, Mr. Hammer, you look a little suspicious dragging a trunk full of whips and chains from the crime scene."

Hammer angrily stood up. "That's enough," he shouted. "I am not saying another word until I talk to my attorney."

"Suit yourself. I am in no hurry. We will talk more tomorrow after you have had a chance to visit with your attorney and enjoy the comforts of our jail."

When Hunter arrived back at his office an elderly black woman was fidgeting with her purse in the hall.

"Detective Hunter, I'm Shirley Jones. I work at Delphi University. They told me you were in charge of the investigation of Dr. Elly's murder. I need to tell you something. It may be nothing, but it's gnawing at me."

"Have a seat Ms. Jones? Can I get you some coffee or a soda?"

"No, I'm fine—just a little nervous."

"Take your time."

"Well, two nights before Dr. Elly was killed I was working my usual shift. It was about 7 pm, and I was cleaning the men's bathroom on the third floor when I heard all this commotion."

"What kind of commotion?"

"People shouting, people running?" "I was scared, so I just peeked around the door. And that's when I saw Professor Savage chasing a woman down the hall. I know Professor Savage, because he works a lot at night."

"Did you recognize the woman?"

"No, sir, but, I am pretty sure it was Dr. Elly?"

"Why is that?"

"When the woman got away, Professor Savage shouted after her, 'Elly, I will kill you, bitch!'"

"Did you report this incident to anyone else, Ms. Jones?"

"No, sir. I didn't want to get involved in no business of white people. After Dr. Elly was killed, my husband told me that I had no choice."

"Ms. Jones, you did the right thing. I need to summarize what you just told me in a written report that I would like you to sign. Is that okay?"

"Will Professor Savage find out that I ratted on him?" Ms. Jones asked nervously.

"Only if he is charged with murder. Then you might have to testify at his trial. However, at this point there is no need for me to mention your name when I question Professor Savage or anyone else."

"Thank you, sir, but I still am a little scared."

"I understand, but try not to worry. I don't think you are in any danger, Ms. Jones. Here is my card. Feel free to call me any time if you think of anything else or just want to talk. Everything is going to be okay."

"Thank you, sir."

"You're welcome. Now let's find someone to take your statement."

Graham left Ms. Jones with the stenographer and returned to his office to review the Elly case in light of her testimony. Had Savage totally flipped and murdered Margo Elly? He had clearly been under a lot of pressure, and Maria's files indicated that he was capable of violent rages. Regardless of whether Savage was the murderer or not, Graham was going to enjoy watching him squirm while he interrogated him.

CHAPTER 30:
MIKE HAMMER OCTOBER 17

In his cell Mike Hammer lay in a fetal position on the bed facing the wall so that none of the other prisoners could see him crying. He knew he was facing a murder charge, but he was more afraid of the damage that the newspapers would do to Margo's reputation if the details of their sex life were revealed. Then he thought about how embarrassed his parents would be and how ashamed he would feel around them. Why hadn't he thrown out the sex toys in the trunk months ago? After all he and Margo hadn't had sex in over a year.

The collapse of Mike and Margo's marriage had been gradual; there had been no major confrontations, just the inevitable outcome of an impossible match between two radically different souls. Mike reminisced about the early days of their courtship. He was a grunt working in the animal lab of the university. She was a new assistant professor. It was one of the few times in his life that he had taken a chance and not worried about rejection. He asked Professor Elly for a date. To his surprise Margo had said "yes." In the early days their mutual fears of loneliness had been enough to overcome their obvious differences.

Unlike many couples Margo and Mike never competed against each other. Mike cared little about professional success and drifted from job to job. Margo, on the other hand, wanted to be the best in her field. She refused to become pregnant or adopt a child. This had been a huge disappointment to Mike. To sublimate his desire for his own children he had dedicated hundreds of hours to coaching both boys and girls soccer. His teams had won numerous championships, but Margo had never seen any of them play. She had no time for childish games.

Mike's move to the second floor of the house mirrored the failure of the marriage. There was no dramatic confrontation. Their different cleanliness standards had always been a problem, but early in their marriage they had been more tolerant of each other. Margo had always insisted on separate bathrooms, but she was more than willing to let Mike turn an upstairs bedroom into his den where he could be a slob. In return Mike had made a special effort to keep their bedroom floor free of his dirty clothes and he never touched Margo's sacred books.

However, as they drifted apart and led their separate lives, Mike began spending more time in his den where he often fell asleep in his recliner. Rather than risking Margo's fury by climbing into bed at 3 am, he began sleeping in the second floor guest room (now his bedroom). Margo didn't protest this change in sleeping arrangements; she welcomed it. Although they continued to have sex once a week, it was no longer spontaneous and passionate. It had become more a way to avoid confrontation than to show affection.

Two years ago, a week prior to their tenth anniversary, Mike had taken a desperate, but sincere, gamble to revive their marriage. He sent Margo a note inviting her to a romantic dinner. If she would cook, he would bring the wine and romance. Margo had responded favorably and had prepared a delicious dinner of chicken marsala, green beans, and roasted potatoes. The evening which had begun in the dining room with candle light and much wine progressed to the living room rug where Margo had never been so passionate. Mike had seized the moment and carried her to bed. Playfully he placed her left wrist in the handcuffs that he had hidden under the pillow. Margo had acted her part perfectly. "If I am going to be your bitch, master, you must totally conquer me." After he had secured both wrists to the headboard, Mike performed oral sex on his partner; Margo expressed more pleasure than he had ever witnessed before. Once her orgasm had subsided, she took command. "Now you will be my love slave," she said. It was now Mike's turn to be handcuffed.

The lust that they had experienced that night was not enough to rekindle their relationship on other fronts. They continued to live separate lives except on Saturday nights. Now Margo would only have sex with Mike if it involved bondage. She had been the one who had created the special sex chamber and purchased all of the S & M paraphernalia. Initially greater control was enough to give her pleasure. Shackles for the ankles and a gag over the mouth had been sufficient, but eventually Margo was unable to reach orgasm unless she was inflicting pain. He knew it was sick, but Mike agreed to wear the dog collar and let his wife strike him across the butt with the whip. It scared him when he realized that Margo's climax was in response to his shouts of pain and the sight of his blood. Nevertheless, he always consented to her deviance, because she would bribe him with a blow job. Mike abruptly ended their Saturday night trysts when Margo asked him to take the role of punisher. She pleaded with him to whip her until she came. The idea of beating her, or anyone for that matter, repulsed him. He had never laid a hand on her in ten years of marriage, even though he often felt tremendous rage towards her. Still bleeding from the lashes that she had unleashed on him, Mike opened his arms to Margo and tried to hold her. She would not be comforted; she bolted from him and cursed him as she ran up the stairs and sought refuge in her bathroom. It had been over a year since that fateful encounter. Neither Mike nor Margo had dared to discuss that incident or anything else in their marriage. They both knew the relationship was comatose.

CHAPTER 31:
GRAHAM HUNTER OCTOBER 18

Mike Hammer's attorney was waiting for Hunter when he arrived at the station the next day. "Where do things stand now?" asked the lawyer.

"Your client was caught removing evidence from the scene of the crime, so that charge will definitely be filed. He is also a suspect in the murder of his wife."

Kevin O'Rourke joined Hunter for the interview. Hunter pressed the record button on the tape recorder and looked directly at Hammer. "As you know, sir, we are investigating the murder of your wife. Can you tell me where you were between the hours of 9 pm on October 6 and 5 am on October 7?"

"I was at my high school reunion in Chicago until midnight. Then I returned to my parents' house in Chicago and spent the night."

"What time did you leave Chicago?"

"Around 8 am."

"Can anyone verify that?"

"I don't think so. My parents went to work before I left. I called their neighbors, but none of them remember seeing me leave."

"Mr. Hammer, I think you left Chicago shortly after midnight. That would have left you plenty of time to drive to Delphi, sneak into your house, kill your wife, and stage the rape scene. Then you took a nice nap in your car somewhere until it was time to return home, discover your dead wife, and assume the role of the grieving husband."

"You can't be serious," angrily shouted Hammer.

"Mr. Hammer, let's not play games. It's pretty clear from even a casual observation of your house that you and your wife were not getting along very well. She lived on the first floor and you resided on the second; that hardly seems like the normal living arrangements for a happily married couple."

"No, you're right. We had drifted apart over the years, but I didn't kill her. I still loved her. I wanted our marriage to work. That's why I didn't move out."

"You still hoped that your S & M trysts might resume again," needled Hunter.

"Fuck you, detective! I am not going to talk with you or anybody else about our sex life. It's none of your damn business."

Hammer's lawyer interrupted, "Detective, I don't see how this line of questioning is relevant."

"Motive," Hunter responded. "Mr. Hammer and the victim had been into some pretty kinky sex in the past. However, given all of the dust and mold in the torture chamber I don't think they had whipped each other into ecstasy for quite some time. Isn't that right Mr. Hammer?"

Hammer stood up abruptly and pounded his fist on the table, "This interview is over. I won't let you smear Margo's reputation by turning this into a sexual perversion case."

Hunter kept up his harangue. "Mr. Hammer, have you forgotten how we found your wife. This has been a sex case from the start. Your little trunk of whips and chains just adds to the mystery. We have no choice but to pursue the sexual deviance angle."

Mike Hammer quickly lost his bravado and slumped back into his chair. "Detective, I'm sorry I got hot, but, please, keep our sex life out of the newspapers for Margo's sake. It has nothing to do with the case."

"How can you be so sure? Maybe your wife found a new partner for her S & M fantasies and things got out of control while you were out of town."

"Detective, you are a real son-of-a-bitch. You want to castrate me as well as convict me of murder."

"Sorry, Mr. Hammer, but we have to pursue every possibility. Did you have any suspicions that your wife might be seeing someone else?"

"You're barking up the wrong tree, detective. Margo didn't have a lover."

"Let's change topics. Do you know if your wife had any enemies at the university?"

"Detective, we didn't talk much about her work?"

Hammer's lawyer then declared, "Detective, you don't have enough evidence to convince the prosecutor to file a murder charge, so why not release my client on his own recognizance?"

"Sorry, counselor, I intend to hold your client for the entire time that I am permitted. Then we will see what the prosecutor and the judge say about bail."

Hunter and O'Rourke left Mike Hammer with his attorney and walked to Hunter's office. "Well, Kevin, what do you think?"

"I am not sure. It's possible that he left Chicago in the middle of the night and killed his wife, but he seems too defeated and broken down to plan and pull off a murder."

"Don't be so sure. Often sex and jealousy can trump depression and lethargy and provide sufficient energy for a rejected lover to kill."

"What are you going to do with Hammer? You know that the judge is going to release him."

"I know, but maybe if he stews a little longer in his cell, he will come up with some other suspects for us."

"Do you really think that Dr. Elly had a lover?"

"Right now I don't know what to think. I want you and O'Malley to remain undercover at the university. Start asking the students questions about Dr. Elly as well as Primal Man. I still need to interview Savage and Spearman."

Justin Mather was waiting for Hunter when he returned to his office.

"Well, Graham, have you finally done your duty and apprehended Dr. Elly's murderer?"

"Justin, you are one annoying SOB. It's only been ten days since Elly's death. Give me a break. Mr. Hammer is a prime suspect, but we have no forensic evidence or eyewitness testimony that links him to the crime."

"So, Sherlock, what's your next move?"

"Justin, if you don't back off, punching you in the nose will be my next move. Now get out!"

"A little more respect for the county prosecutor, detective, or you might find yourself walking the beat again."

Graham angrily rose from his desk and Mather made a hasty retreat into the safety of the Delphi streets. Still incensed Hunter reviewed his thirty year battle with Mather. The animosity had begun in their freshman year of high school. Mather had been the goalie on the Delphi High soccer team. Graham had been the star forward for St. John Bosco, the local Catholic high school. Mather's team never beat John Bosco during their four years of high school, and in every game Graham had managed to score at least one goal off his enemy. A non-declared cease-fire had existed for seven years while Mather pursued his undergraduate and law degrees at Regents University. The battle had resumed when Mather returned to Delphi and decided to run for county prosecutor on the Republican ticket. Hunter openly supported his Democratic opponent. He used his police and youth soccer connections to raise money, pass out flyers, and drive people to the polls. Mather narrowly won the election, but he never forgot that his old nemesis had publicly opposed him. The contempt that the two foes had for each other was based on more than politics and adolescent jealousy. Mather was a fundamentalist in all aspects of life, particularly religion and the law. Hunter, on the other hand, was much more interested in promoting social justice than defending a literal interpretation of the Bible or the Constitution.

CHAPTER 32:
MARIA FLORES OCTOBER 19

Maria had not seen Hunter since Dr. Elly's funeral. She decided to invite him for dinner to discuss recent developments in the investigation. For this rendezvous Maria held nothing back. The table was set with candles and Frank Sinatra crooned in the background. She made the bed with her best satin sheets and had votive candles ready to light when the time came. She wore her tightest fitting jeans and the purple v-neck sweater that always held Hunter's attention. For the finishing touch she dabbed herself with Poison by Christian Dior.

Maria had just finished preparing dinner when the doorbell rang. She greeted Hunter with a gentle hand squeeze and immediately noticed that he was wearing Polo cologne. This was definitely more than a business meeting. Hunter opened the bottle of Pinot Grigio while Maria was bringing dinner to the table. She could sense Hunter's nervous excitement as she lit candles on the table. The chicken Mirabella was perfect as was the jasmine flavored rice, cut green beans, and apricot tart. During the meal Maria questioned Graham about his progress in the Elly case, particularly his recent interrogation of Hammer. She still considered Primal Man and Savage the prime suspects. She could not conceive of Hammer killing his wife after she saw his grief at the funeral. Graham was not so sure.

Maria was at the kitchen sink rinsing the dishes when Graham made his move. He simply walked up behind her and kissed her on the neck. Maria turned and responded with a full wet kiss for her new lover. The couple retired to the living room where they slow danced to the music of Sinatra for an hour. Then Maria affectionately led Graham to the bed with the virgin satin sheets.

Maria's slumber did not last long. She gazed at the Yanquee cop beside her and began doubting the wisdom of her actions. Unable to fall back asleep she went to the kitchen to make coffee. As she sipped her café con leche she could not stop her mind from comparing Graham to the previous men in her life. There had not been many. A few had been as intelligent as Graham; one had been even more handsome than the Yanquee cop. However, none of them had made her feel like this.

Maria looked around her living room. The artifacts in the room proudly displayed her heritage. Two large art books lay on the table. One contained photos and information about Machu Picchu. The other exhibited sites in Chile including: the majestic Andes, the ports of Antofagasta and Valpariso, the resorts of Vina del Mar and Zapallar, and the black beaches of the lake near Pucon. Prominently displayed in her bookcase were books by Pablo Neruda and Isabel Allende. Covering her silk pajamas was her favorite red and black poncho from the Argentine province of Salta. However, she was no longer a Chilean journalist; she was a reporter for a Yanquee newspaper. Although she still had one foot planted in South America, her infatuation with the shy gringo was pulling her more toward the US. Maria's reminiscences were interrupted by a kiss on the back of her neck by the shy gringo.

"Are you okay? he asked. "You look sad."

"Not sad, just preoccupied. Come closer." She kissed him gently on the lips and held his hand. "I have been thinking about last night and the future. I don't make it a habit of going to bed with someone about whom I know so little. Last night was terrific, but there can't be another one until I learn more about you. I don't even know if you are married, or more importantly, whether you are a Democrat or Republican. God, I hope I didn't make love to a Republican! I think that I would kill myself."

"Maria, no need to be suicidal. I have never been married. And, I have always voted Democratic."

"Let's get some more coffee. Then we can tell each other our life stories." Fortified by fresh coffee Maria slyly implored, "Graham, you go first. You're my guest."

"Okay. I'll start with the demographics. I am the oldest of six children (all Caesarean)."

"So, you must be Catholic?"

"I am a 'recovering Catholic.' I was baptized Catholic, but I lost my faith long ago. I no longer go to Church, nor do I subscribe to its dogma. However, my religous upbringing will always haunt me."

"Tell me about your family."

"My parents are both dead. My father emigrated from Liverpool, England; my mother came from County Cork, Ireland. They were classmates in high school. My father was smitten with my mother's good looks, especially her fair skin and long black hair. My mother admired my father's athletic prowess on the soccer field, but she was more impressed by his good manners and the fact that he didn't drink. She was disgusted with the heavy drinking of the Irish men. They dated for two years and were married at age twenty. They had six children within a span of twelve years. I am the oldest, then Bridget, Kathleen, Clive, Coleen, and Harry."

"Irish names for the girls and English names for the boys—interesting compromise."

"Maria, now it's your turn."

"You know that I left Chile shortly after Allende was assassinated. I had just graduated from journalism school and was working for a newspaper that was supportive of Allende. Left wing reporters were obvious targets for Pinochet and his fellow murderers. I had to leave or risk imprisonment. Fortunately, I had friends in the American embassy that helped me obtain a visa. I ended up coming to Delphi, because my boss in Chile had been a classmate of the Scribe's editor."

"And your family?"

"They all remained in Chile. I also am from a large Catholic family. There are five boys (Luis, Ignacio, Miguel, Santiago, and Hector) and four girls (myself, Teresa, Isabel, and Martina). I am the middle child; that is why I am so loveable and easy to get along with!"

"Are your parents still living?"

Maria's eyes became red and a tear rolled down her cheek. "No, they both died of cancer. I was not even able to attend their funerals—yet another atrocity perpetrated by Pinochet and his henchmen. It was too risky for me to travel to Chile."

Graham wiped away the tear and held her hand. "I am so sorry. Do you want to continue?"

"Yes, I have to. I can't be your lover without being your friend, and friends tell each other everything."

Maria and Graham spent the rest of the day walking through the Elysian Fields and the Olympic Forest learning each other's history. Maria was not surprised that Graham was a star soccer player, but she was stunned to learn that he was a pacifist and a student of philosophy. Graham learned that Maria had studied art history as well as journalism in college, and that she spent as much time as she could in museums viewing art. Her only regret was that she somehow had never been able to summon the courage to paint herself. She considered her fear of plunging into the creative process a major character flaw. She vowed someday to overcome her phobia. The two lovers discovered that they both liked ethnic food, old films, Joan Baez, Bob Dylan, and mysteries. The evening was a repeat of the previous night's experience (dinner, Sinatra, dirty dancing, and early to bed).

CHAPTER 33:
GRAHAM HUNTER OCTOBER 21

Hunter awoke remarkably refreshed. Quietly he slipped out of bed and made his way to the precinct. Usually a case like the Elly murder would seize his mind and his body until it was solved. His sleep would be constantly interrupted with nightmares or some new insight into the investigation. During these periods Graham became so absorbed in the case that he lost contact with the rest of life. He stopped watching television, reading books, or going to movies. Even his olfactory and gustatory senses seemed to stop functioning; he no longer could savor the food and drink that passed his lips. Maria Flores had changed all that.

Hunter was looking forward to interviewing Savage. He relished the idea of watching the scum bag squirm, even if the interrogation did not produce enough evidence for an indictment. Although Savage had initially refused to come down to the station for an interview, he grudgingly acquiesced when Hunter threatened to show up at his office with handcuffs. Hunter kept him waiting for thirty minutes in the hottest and starkest interview room while he finished his third cup of coffee and a second glazed donut.

"Professor Savage, do you want an attorney present before we begin?"

"I don't need an attorney. Ask your, questions, detective."

"If you change your mind, just let me know. When did you last see Dr. Elly?"

"Gee, Detective, I don't know. I rarely saw her. Our offices are in different buildings."

"Come on, Savage. We know she came to your office two days before she was killed; you were seen chasing her down the hall. Shall we start there?"

"Sorry, detective. I had nothing to do with her death. I was just trying to spare myself some grief. Here's the whole story. I had been seeing one of Elly's research assistants. She was furious about it, particularly because Emily, her assistant, had decided to forego a fellowship at Harvard in biochemistry to study sociobiology and live with me. Elly came to my office one Friday night and threatened me. I lost my head, screamed at her, and chased her down the hall."

"How did she threaten you?"

"She said that if I didn't convince Emily to accept the Harvard fellowship, she was going to go after me on sexual harassment charges."

"Did she have a case?"

"Not really. All of my partners have been over eighteen and very willing; however, defending myself could have been ugly and expensive. I was pissed, but I didn't kill her."

"Any communication with Dr. Elly after that night?"

"No."

"Can you tell me where you were between 10 pm on October 6 and 5 am on October 7?"

"Sure, I was home."

"Can anyone verify that?"

"Yeah, the kids who live across the hall. They were having a party and I told them to quiet down."

Hunter tossed a phone book at Savage. "Names and phone numbers."

Savage scribbled the information Hunter had asked for and handed it to him. "Anything else, detective?"

"Yes. Do you have any idea who the campus flasher is? Given the Primal Man moniker, he must have taken at least one of your classes."

"Sorry, detective, I wish I did. The little pervert has caused me a lot of grief."

"I think you got it all wrong, Professor. Your sexist horseshit has turned some mixed-up kid into a pervert."

Savage's face became flushed and he clenched his fist. Then he took a deep breath and relaxed. "Detective, I'm not going to take the bait. The campus flasher is your responsibility, not mine."

"When are you scheduled to leave for Africa?"

"November 1."

"I wouldn't pack your bags yet. There is a strong possibility that Judge Solomon will want you to stay in Delphi until this crime is solved. Don't be sad, Georgie," chided Hunter sarcastically. "The delay will give you more time to spend with Professor German."

"Fuck you!"

"No thanks. One last piece of advice. Get yourself an attorney. I don't think this will be our last man-to-man chat."

After a quick lunch at Hardees, Hunter decided to spend the afternoon visiting with Jacob Spearman. The once promising herpetologist was now a salesman for a medical supply company. His office was located in one of the numerous strip malls that scar the American landscape. This particular one had seen better days. Tenants included a massage parlor, resale shop, pawn shop, topless bar, Chinese take-out place, and Jones Medical Supply. Security was an obvious concern, as Graham had to identify himself on an intercom and look into a security camera before he was buzzed in. Sally Heater, the receptionist, looked liked an extra from the movie *Grease*. Her teased platinum hair smelled of cheap hair spray; her lips were painted pale pink and her eyes were adorned with purple eye shadow and too much mascara; she wore tight fitting Capri pants and a blouse that was buttoned and tied to expose maximum cleavage and her navel.

"Jake, someone to see you," shouted Miss Heater.

"Send him in," grunted Spearman.

The office was a cluttered mess. Supply catalogues were strewn all over the place; boxes of supplies were piled everywhere. It was obvious that Spearman's office was also his warehouse. A TV, video tape player, and a stack of adult videos sat on a wobbly stand across from a plaid couch. Hunter had no doubt that the couch could quickly become a bed if the right opportunity presented itself.

Spearman had the John Travolta *Saturday Night Fever* look. He wore tight fitting pants that were flared at the bottom and a disco shirt that was buttoned closer to the navel than the neck, exposing a hairy chest and gold medallion. His hair was dyed jet black and slicked back to cover a sizable bald spot.

Graham flashed his badge and introduced himself. "I am investigating the murder of Margo Elly."

"What's that have to do with me? I haven't seen her in over five years."

"Motive! You are on our list of people who might have wanted to see Dr. Elly dead. We know that Dr. Elly was very instrumental in your dismissal from the university."

"No question about it. She ruined my life. She was a frustrated hag who couldn't stay out of other people's lives. I never raped any of those students or gave them good grades based on their sexual performance. I simply gave those young women what they wanted—great sex from an experienced lover. I don't mourn the passing of the Ice Queen, but I didn't kill her."

"You said you hadn't seen Dr. Elly in over five years. How about contact through letter, phone, or email?"

"No, nothing."

"Are you sure, Mr. Spearman?"

"Yes, I'm sure. I vowed never to give the bitch the satisfaction of knowing how much she screwed up my life. Not only did I lose my job, but I lost my wife and my son because of her. My wife was so humiliated and angry that she immediately moved to Minnesota after the scandal hit the newspaper. Yeah, I am bitter, but I am not stupid. After Elly filed the complaint against me, I never communicated with the Ice Queen again. I let my lawyer do all of the talking."

"How do you explain this email?"

"It's a fake. I wouldn't give Elly the satisfaction of knowing that I still hated her."

"That's precisely the point. You do still hate her and welcomed her death. Now let's talk about opportunity. Can you tell me where you were between the hours of 10 pm October 6 and 5 am October 7?"

"I was getting hammered and salivating at a plethora of tits and ass at Club Erotica."

"Any witnesses?"

"The bartender, Jim Burke. I'm a regular. Any other questions?"

"Just, one. Any thoughts about who else might have wanted to see Dr. Elly dead?"

"I suspect that's a long list, but I can't think of anyone with the balls to take the risk. Academics are wimps. They are more likely to retaliate with memos and novels than take up arms."

Spearman escorted Hunter to the waiting room where Ms. Heater had just finished painting her nails a brilliant purple which matched her eye shadow. As Hunter walked out the door he glanced back to see Spearman grab Ms. Heater from behind and crudely yank down her panties. Sally whirled and slapped him so hard that his face turned scarlet. "What's wrong with you Jake? You know you can have my ass or any other part of my body whenever you want, but you gotta be nice. That wasn't love making; that was attempted rape. I'm outta here."

Spearman made no attempt to stop her or explain his actions. Some guys never learn, thought Hunter. I had better get my suit cleaned. Who knows what kind of microbes live and multiply in that couch?

Jacob Spearman was easy to dislike; he was crude, egotistical, and lacked any moral fiber. However, he seemed too narcissistic to risk jail in seeking his revenge on Margo Elly. Nevertheless, Hunter would have Kevin O'Rourke check out his alibi. And for the pure pleasure of rattling him, Graham decided to seek a search warrant for Spearman's office. Although he suspected that his porno collection was entirely legal, there was no harm in conducting a more detailed investigation to protect the citizens of Delphi!

Graham arrived home around 6:30 pm. Tonight's cuisine consisted of a large burrito and two tacos from Taco Bell. Hunter now had four suspects: Primal Man, George Savage, Jacob Spearman, and Mike Hammer. All had motive and opportunity to murder Margo Elly, but not a single piece of evidence could place any of them at the scene of the crime. Graham was stuck; he had no idea how to proceed. Empiricism, the scientific method, his training, and his experience had all failed him. He reviewed Kant's scheme for understanding reality. The philosopher acknowledged the position of the empiricists that observation by the senses was the only way man could know another object. He also agreed that consensus across observers provided more certitude that an object was real. However, Kant also proposed that the object itself has its own identity, the nomena, which the observer could never completely know. Hunter's own experience supported Kant's position; it was impossible to completely comprehend another's thoughts or feelings. He suspected that Kant's dualistic formulation was rooted in his belief that humans have a soul that is independent of the physical body. Even though modern science no longer talked about a soul or made a distinction between mind and body, humans still seemed to have a need to believe that they were somehow more than their bodies. Mentally exhausted Graham began laughing at himself; his rehash of Kant added absolutely nothing to his investigation. However, studying the great philosophers was never a waste of time.

CHAPTER 34:
GRAHAM HUNTER OCTOBER 23

Kevin O'Rourke was waiting for Hunter when he arrived at his office. "Primal Man struck again last night, Graham. He flashed Dr. German."

"Kevin, you must be joking. Surely Primal Man didn't have the balls to flash the general of the New Amazons?"

"I am afraid he did. Dr. German gave a perfect description of the culprit, including the orange condom."

Hunter took the 3 x 5 index card from Kevin's outstretched hand and read, "German, if you don't want to end up like Dr. Elly, abandon your crusade against Professor Savage and PMS!"

"Is she okay?"

"Why don't you ask her yourself? She's in the waiting room."

Hilda German marched into Hunter's office in her military fatigues. She did not display any body language indicating that Primal Man had traumatized her. Quite the contrary, the incident merely annoyed and angered her. She dismissed Hunter's offer of sexual assault counseling.

"Dr. German, Detective O'Rourke gave me an overview of your encounter with Primal Man. I only have a few follow-up questions. Why did you risk being on campus at 11:30 pm last night?"

"Detective, I needed something from the library, and I refuse to let some pervert impinge upon my freedom."

"I see. Now would you please describe your entire interaction with the perpetrator. Take your time. The details may be important."

"I was in the library parking lot when the little twerp emerged from behind a car and opened his raincoat and began shaking his orange clad thing at me. I called him a coward and dared him to come closer. He opened his mouth as if he was trying to say something, but no sound came out. When I moved toward him with my cane raised, the little weasel simply threw the index card at me and scampered into the forest with the other animals. If I didn't have this bum knee, I would have castrated the little prick with my cane."

"Thanks, Dr. German; your description is very helpful. One last question, why did you wait until this morning to report the crime?"

"To be honest, detective, I wasn't going to tell anyone about the incident. I didn't want to give the puny bastard the satisfaction of seeing his name in the paper again, but my best friend convinced me that I might be endangering more women by not reporting the crime. So here I am. Detective, you had better catch this slime-ball fast, or the New Amazons will take action."

Hunter was vexed. He felt his stomach tighten, but he maintained his professional demeanor. "Dr. German, I am warning you; do not take the law into your own hands. If you initiate any type of vigilante operation, I will come down on you hard. This is police business. If you want to do something positive, use the New Amazons as escorts for women around campus."

Slowly German rose from the chair and glared at Hunter. "Then do your job, detective, and catch the little prick!" With that exchange the interview ended.

After Dr. German left his office, Hunter stood up, slowly stretched his arm into the air, and then violently pounded his desk in frustration. He was too agitated to sit, so he left the precinct building and walked toward the Lethe River. Unfortunately, this time the tranquil murmur of the river flowing toward the Mississippi did not soothe his temper or help him forget his problems. Initially Graham suspected that German had fabricated her story, but she could not have known about the orange condom. Hunter had hoped that the campus flasher would retreat to his cave, but instead Primal Man was getting bolder. No longer was he flashing his orange spear at random co-eds. This time he picked a specific target, the leader of the New Amazons no less. His note had issued a threat against German and once again referred directly to the Elly murder. In addition, this was the second time that he had unsuccessfully tried to speak to his victim. Although most exhibitionists rarely became violent, Primal Man appeared to be a different kind of animal. Hunter feared that his choice of particular targets and his inability to verbally confront them made him more and more dangerous. He had to be caught soon.

CHAPTER 35:
MARIA FLORES OCTOBER 23

Once Maria Flores learned of the latest flashing incident she rushed to the police station. Unable to locate Hunter she spent the afternoon trying to pull information from Kevin O'Rourke and Kathy O'Malley, but the two officers were tight-lipped and referred her to detective Hunter. Maria decided that her only option was to wait for Hunter at her apartment. They had a 7 pm dinner date. She was cooking Chilean sea bass. Graham finally arrived at 7:30, apologetic but preoccupied.

"What's wrong?" asked Maria sympathetically.

"I can't talk about it," Graham responded tersely.

"A little touchy, aren't we? Graham, you must learn to be more trusting, particularly with the woman who, and I quote, 'gives you more pleasure than a freezer full of chocolate chip ice cream.'"

Graham took Maria's hand and apologized with his eyes. "Sorry, the Elly case is becoming a nightmare for me. I don't know where the boundaries should be between our personal and professional lives. I don't want to screw-up our relationship by clamming up, but police procedures and ethics all require some limits. This is all so new. I'm just confused."

Maria kissed Graham gently on the lips. "Let's have dinner and some good Chilean wine. Then we can talk about professional ethics and boundaries. Although I am a pushy, nosey journalist, I don't want to jeopardize our relationship either. You are the best thing that has happened to me in a long time."

Bach's Partita Number Two provided the background music for the dinner and a long discussion and negotiation regarding professional ethics. The music was majestic and soothing at the same time.

The next morning Maria slowly dragged herself out of bed; she was not a morning person. Graham had left hours ago for a meeting with O'Rourke. As she sipped her café con leche she reviewed the professional boundaries agreement that she and Graham had negotiated the night before. Maria would not press Graham for any insider information, but she was free to pursue other informants, including other police officers. The most important commitment that they made was never to lie. "No comment" was declared an acceptable response with no negative repercussions in bed or elsewhere.

Although the ground rules made theoretical sense, upon more reflection Maria knew that they were not practical. She could not be a good crime reporter without violating her agreement. Conflicts were inevitable between crime reporters who crave every bit of new information regarding a case and detectives who are trying to withhold information until they have all the evidence needed to prosecute a case. Maria also knew that her daily presence at the Delphi police station was going to make life difficult for both Graham and her once their relationship became public. Already her co-workers suspected something. Everyone kept commenting on "how satisfied" she looked during the past few weeks.

Maria was hopelessly in love with the Yanquee cop. He was the most sensitive man that she had ever met, and he was not bad looking. His deep-set eyes and full lips were his best features. His only negative characteristic was his paunch, but a strict diet and more exercise could fix that issue. Her main problem with Graham was his job—or her job, depending on your point of view. Maria needed a new plan for both her professional and personal life. After a half hour walk on Minerva's Trail she had a solution to her dilemma. She would ask her editor to switch her beat from the Delphi police department to Delphi University. This would remove the potential conflicts that both she and Graham dreaded. Although she would miss the adrenaline rush that was associated with getting the scoop on a major crime investigation, she looked forward to the opportunity to conduct more in depth investigations on Margo Elly, George Savage, the New Amazons, and Darwin's Disciples.

Maria decided that researching the life of Margo Elly was the first story that she would pursue. Graham had given her a copy of Elly's CV which provided some leads with regard to her professional life. Maria was more intrigued by Elly's personal life which remained an enigma. The journalist had been struck by the paucity of faculty and students who had attended the funeral. She was even more curious about Margo Elly's family. Even cold-hearted Yanquees assembled for family weddings and funerals. She wondered if her parents were still alive, or if she had any siblings. She also wanted to follow-up on her brief conversation with Melissa Hope. There was something more to the relationship between Elly and Hope.

CHAPTER 36:
PRIMAL MAN OCTOBER 24

Proudly Primal Man read the account of his latest mission on the front page of the *Scribe*. He had carefully stalked his prey, waiting for the moment that he could confront the prime persecutor of Professor Savage. German had become his number one enemy. She had to be stopped. For three days he had carried his uniform in his backpack, ready to transform himself when the opportunity came. Then the skinny slut decided to go to the library late at night. The parking lot was close to the woods and nearly empty, so there was little danger of being caught. While his quarry was in the library he quickly resurrected Primal Man. Then when she was almost at her car, he sprang from his hiding place and put the fear of God in her. He only wished that he could have told her how he felt, but the words wouldn't come. Nevertheless, he still had been able to deliver his message. She must abandon her war on Professor Savage and PMS or else.

As the excitement of his latest operation began to fade Primal Man reverted to a lonely college student. He missed his sister. He worried that his mother might be displacing her frustrations with life onto her now that he was not there. He still wondered what his father was up to, but he no longer felt a strong urge to communicate with him. He now loathed his father as much as he hated his mother. They were a pathetic couple who never should have been allowed to have children. He didn't need either of them any more.

Tears rolled from his eyes as he fumbled with the beads of his confirmation rosary. Tonight the sorrowful mysteries were his companion. He knew that Professor Savage would not approve of this superstitious practice, but he could not completely abandon his religion. As a young boy he had wanted to become a priest. He had begun this career pursuit by studying to be an altar boy, but he was not chosen for this honor because of his stutter. The priest claimed that this rejection was for his own protection. "Some sinners in the congregation might hurt your feelings by complaining about your speech impediment as you recite the Mass responses," the priest had said. Denied his chosen vocation he had pursued God in his own private way by praying the rosary daily and collecting holy cards of his favorite saints. However, in recent years he often felt abandoned by his God and looked for salvation elsewhere. PMS was his most recent candidate to replace Catholicism, but no matter how hard he tried he could not free himself from the religion of his birth. After reciting the rosary the confused student fell asleep.

CHAPTER 37:
FATHER DOMINIC OCTOBER 25

Father Dominic sat alone in the sacristy after saying Mass. Performing the sacraments was normally the highlight of his day, but lately he was just going through the motions. He doubted whether he was really transforming the bread and wine into the body and blood of Christ during the consecration. He even questioned the essential doctrine of the Church, namely that Jesus Christ had died for the sins of mankind and had been resurrected from the dead. He also had doubts about the goodness of God. The priest could accept that war, poverty, and other human suffering were consequences of man's free will. However, he could not understand how a loving and just God could permit so many people to lose their lives in floods, earthquakes, and other natural disasters. Perhaps the Gnostics were right after all. Maybe there were two gods, an evil god and a good god, who were in a constant battle. Similarly, many cultures, including the Greeks and the Egyptians, had multiple deities that competed with each other.

The recent chaos on the Delphi University campus had only exacerbated Father Dominic's crisis of faith. He had prayed fervently for guidance, but his prayers went unanswered. For no apparent reason he decided to seek the counsel of the Oracle. The priestess smiled modestly and escorted him to the inner sanctum. The smell of burning tar rose from the grates and almost choked the priest.

"How can I help you, Father?"

"How can I bring peace to Delphi University?"

"You must extinguish the fires of fanaticism."

Father Dominic knew the Oracle was right, but he had no insight into how to end the intolerance that permeated his university.

CHAPTER 38:
GRAHAM HUNTER OCTOBER 25

Today Hunter was arresting George Savage for the murder of Margo Elly. He had informed Maria, so that she could tape Savage's reactions as he passed the demonstrators. When Hunter arrived, the New Amazons stood on the sidewalk chanting their slogan, "Savage, Savage, you're a knave. You and Primal Man belong in a cave."

Graham rang the doorbell; a disheveled Savage peered out the window. When he opened the door Hunter flashed his badge and announced that he was under arrest for the murder of Margo Elly. After cuffing his suspect Hunter escorted the director of the PMS through the gauntlet of German's soldiers shouting their slogan and waving their "STOP PMS NOW" signs. In the confined space of the patrol car Hunter nearly choked on Savage's stench. His breath reeked of cheap whiskey and his body gave off a pungent aroma of decayed meat. As the patrol car inched forward, Hunter spotted Maria's blue 87 Honda Accord; her window was down and her video camera was rolling. Savage also noticed the journalist and grumbled, "Detective, you're a real SOB. You tipped off the spic reporter of my arrest. I'm going to sue your ass when this is over."

At the station Savage was finger printed, stripped searched, sprayed with a strong smelling disinfectant, and pushed into a cold shower by a sadistic guard. After donning an orange prison jumpsuit he was escorted to his cell. It had two beds, an open toilet, and a tiny sink. Still hung-over Savage collapsed on the lower bunk; within minutes he was snoring deeply. An hour later Hunter went to the cellblock to retrieve the suspect. Savage was rolling on the floor screaming in terror.

"Bad dream?" asked one of the guards.

"Yeah."

"Well, I don't think you are going to like reality much better. Detective Hunter wants to interview you."

When they arrived at the interrogation room Kathy O'Malley and Savage's attorney were already assembled. After activating the tape recorder Hunter nodded toward O'Malley to begin the questioning.

"Professor Savage, do you remember our encounter last year in the parking lot of the Dionysius Wine Bar?"

"How could I forget, officer? You made your points quite emphatically."

"And yet you seemed to have forgotten my warning. Tell me about Emily Smith."

"Emily, like all of the women who had the pleasure of my bed, is of legal age."

"Excuse me, sir, but doesn't the university have rules about fornicating with your students?"

"Emily was not enrolled in my class; she was just sitting in."

"Excuse me, officer," interrupted Savage's attorney. "Although having an affair with one of your students may be unwise and against university policy, it is not a crime. Please refrain from asking questions that are not relevant to one of the crimes under investigation."

"Okay, counselor, perhaps your client might be willing to answer some questions about some prior crimes. Let's start with vehicular homicide." Slowly and deliberately O'Malley removed four photos from her file and laid them in front of Savage and his lawyer.

"Officer, what's your point? I don't see the relevance of these photos to the cases under consideration here. Moreover, my client was found innocent of vehicular homicide."

O'Malley remained silent and removed four more photos from another envelope and laid them down for inspection.

"Officer, who are these women?"

"The ex-wives of your client. It seems he has a problem controlling his temper."

"Where did you get those?" demanded an angry Savage.

"A concerned citizen," calmly responded O'Malley.

"I was never charged with anything," Savage pleaded.

"Unfortunately, that is true. Your prior wives were too ashamed to press charges. They simply fled the 'pleasure of your bed' to use your expression."

Once again Savage's lawyer interrupted, "Ms. O'Malley, please stick to the case under investigation. Even an inexperienced officer should know that a judge will not permit these photos or any discussion of prior charges to be presented as evidence in the Elly murder case."

"You may be right, counselor," interrupted Hunter. "However, I am sure that the prosecutor will give it the old college try. At the very least the judge will have an opportunity to see what a kind and gentle person you are defending. Officer O'Malley, if you have finished, I would like to change topics and ask the distinguished Professor about his relationship with Professor Elly."

"Your witness, sir."

"Professor, let's start with your whereabouts on the night of the murder."

"Like I told you before, I was home. Didn't the students who live across the hall verify that I was home that night?"

"Unfortunately, they were all too stoned to remember if they had the pleasure of your countenance on the night in question. Consequently, you have no alibi."

"Lack of an alibi is not sufficient grounds for conviction," interjected Savage's lawyer.

"Agreed, counselor. Shall I move on to motive? Professor Savage, could you describe your relationship with Dr. Elly?"

"Come on, Hunter, you already know that Dr. Elly and I were not the best of friends."

"That's an understatement wouldn't you say? Did you not threaten to kill Dr. Elly on the night of October 4, just days before she was murdered."

"We had an argument about Emily."

"It was a little more than that, George. We have a witness who will testify that you chased Dr. Elly up and down the halls of the Murky Social Science Building, threatening to kill her."

"Well, maybe I did say something in anger like that, but I never struck her."

Graham turned up the heat on the perspiring Savage. "That's only because you were too drunk and fat to catch her. No, you, the cunning cave man, waited a couple of days to stalk your prey. How did you do it, Savage? How did you convince Dr. Elly to let you enter her home? Did you tell her that you had convinced Emily Smith to take the scholarship at Harvard? Did you bring a bottle of wine as a peace offering?"

"Fuck you, detective! I hated the bitch, but I didn't kill her. I don't even know where she lives."

"That's strange, because we lifted your finger prints from a folder in Dr. Elly's home."

"It must have been the folder that Elly shoved in my face the night she visited my office. It contained a list of former students whom Elly was trying to convince to testify against me."

"The folder that we recovered contained one of your articles on gender relationships. Given that your finger prints were the only ones present besides those of the victim, we assumed that you left the article as your calling card."

"Very clever, detective. Do you think that I would be dumb enough to leave such incriminating evidence if I had iced Dr. Elly?"

"Actually, I have serious questions about your intelligence. Anybody who promulgates the sexist bullshit that you espouse seems a little retarded to me."

"Detective, you are badgering my client. Do you have any more questions?"

"Sorry, counselor. I didn't realize Professor Savage had such a delicate constitution. Professor, please review this email correspondence that we removed from Dr. Elly's computer."

"The email from me to Margo Elly is bogus. You can check my office and home computers. I didn't send that message. I did not want to have another battle with the Ice Queen. Someone is trying to frame me."

"And who would want to do that, Professor?"

"You might start with German and the New Amazons."

"Thanks for the tip, but for the time being you are our number one suspect."

"Detective, I find your interview style quite inappropriate. I plan to file a complaint with your commanding officer and the prosecutor. Furthermore, I intend to ask the prosecutor and Judge Solomon to release my client as soon as possible."

Hunter refused to be intimidated by Savage's lawyer. "Counselor, we are both just doing our jobs. I have no doubt that you will secure a temporary reprieve for your client. I also expect that the judge will ask your client to surrender his passport and post a large amount of bail. After all he has already purchased a ticket to Africa which makes him a significant flight risk. Good day."

CHAPTER 39:
HILDA GERMAN OCTOBER 25

Hilda German and the New Amazons had effectively cancelled Savage's course on gender relationships. Most students simply dropped the course, rather than try to listen to the lectures over the now familiar chant of "Savage, Savage . . . ." His teaching assistant tried to hold class in clandestine locations for the few remaining loyalists, but inevitably the New Amazons would find them and resume their harangue. German, however, was not satisfied. She was still angry at President Sinduce for rewarding Savage with a research leave rather than firing him. When Sinduce failed to respond to her request to cancel the PMS program, Hilda became even more enraged. Why couldn't Sinduce and the others see that Primal Man and Margo Elly's murder were both products of the sexist garbage taught in the PMS courses?

The general decided that more drastic actions were needed to permanently crush the PMS program. With the help of Sara Chaste she created the "Feminist Index" which was a list of all the primary and secondary sources used by the PMS faculty and other literature classified as promoting the male chauvinist agenda. Hilda then organized a secret meeting of her most trusted New Amazons. Each Amazon was given a list of books and periodicals to steal from the library and the campus book store. The Feminist index included all the novels written by Henry Miller, Philip Roth, Norman Mailer, John Updike, and Bret Easton Ellis. In addition the following titles were also included:

Sociobiology: The New Synthesis by E. O. Wilson

Evolutionary Psychology: A Primer by L. Cosmides and J. Tooby

The Mating Mind: How Sexual Choices Shaped the Evolution of Human Nature by G.F. Miller.

Survival of the Prettiest: The Science of Beauty by Nancy Etioff

Sophie's Choice by William Styron.

With no books or journal articles it would be difficult for Darwin's Disciples and the PMS program to promulgate their hatred of women under the guise of science. German's plan had been remarkably successful. In a matter of days the New Amazons had stolen nearly all of the offensive literature and had destroyed it in a massive bonfire which was televised on CNN. Chief Gunn's investigation had produced no concrete evidence against Hilda German or any of the New Amazons. All of the book burners had worn Batgirl masks as they danced around the fire and celebrated another victory over the weaker sex. None of Darwin's Disciples or the police had dared to unveil any of the perpetrators for fear of being accused of sexual assault.

The Faculty Senate called for an immediate investigation into the book burning and demanded that all faculty and students involved in this heinous threat to academic freedom be dismissed from the university. The American Association of University Professors issued a similar proclamation and demanded that President Sinduce take quick and decisive action against these self-appointed censors. The Women's Studies faculty was in a difficult position. The organization publicly condemned the book burning, but privately many women faculty members admired German and her New Amazons.

In reaction Darwin's Disciples created their own list of forbidden literature. This catalog included all of the books written by Betty Friedan, Gloria Steinam, Susan Brownmiller, Margaret Atwood, Flannery O'Connor, and Agatha Christie. Also included were the *S.C.U.M (Society for Cutting Up Men) Manifesto* and *Our Bodies, Ourselves*. However, Darwin's Disciples were not nearly as discreet as the New Amazons; nearly every disciple who tried to steal a book was caught. Once again the little boys had been "out-manned" by their more mature sisters.

CHAPTER 40:
MARIA FLORES OCTOBER 28

Maria decided to write two feature articles on Margo Elly. One would focus on her professional development and the other would concentrate on her early life. Dr. Elly's career began as an undergraduate at Missouri State College where she graduated summa cum laude in biology. Professor Jeffrey Jones, her advisor, described her as smart, methodical, dedicated, but aloof. She preferred to work independently, and she never joined the biology club or any other campus organization. Dr. Elly received a graduate fellowship to Harvard University where she earned a Ph.D. in biochemistry. She was considered the most promising student in her class and published several papers before completing her doctorate. Her doctoral advisor, Professor Gregory Munson, described Elly as a loner. He reported that she had few friends and never participated in any of the social events sponsored by the biochemistry department. Hilda German, Judy Lacky, and the public relations director of Smith Pharmaceuticals provided Maria with detailed information on her career at Delphi University. The development of Spermicide Complete and Passion with Protection were clearly her most important successes. Margo Elly's pattern of social isolation continued at Dephi. She spent little time with any of her colleagues in the biochemistry department or the Women's Studies Program. She never held any elective office or attended social events at the university. None of Dr. Elly's students were willing to discuss their relationship with their mentor. However, one of them did reveal that the students' nickname for their professor was "Ice Queen"—queen because she had a haughty, superior attitude toward others, and ice because she was inflexible and lacked warmth.

Maria's investigation of Margo Elly's personal life, particularly her pre-college years, began with an interview of Mike Hammer. Hammer knew little about his wife's life prior to their marriage and refused to discuss their relationship. He did inform the journalist that Elly was an only child who grew up on a farm in the Missouri Bootheel. After considerable searching, Maria found a phone number for Dr. Elly's parents. The phone call was awkward and heartrending. Ethel Elly clearly had not been informed of her daughter's death. After regaining her composure she informed Maria that Margo had cut all communication with her parents after she had graduated from college. Although Mrs. Elly could not comprehend why a reporter would want to talk to her, she consented to an interview.

As Maria drove down I-55 she noticed a change in the landscape as cotton fields replaced corn fields. When she stopped for lunch and saw grits on the menu, Maria knew that she had entered the South. The accents of the other patrons in the restaurant confirmed that she was now in Dixie. Despite the friendliness of the waitress, Maria's own prejudices made her anxious. Would these descendants of the Ku Klux Klan harm her because her skin was brown and she spoke with a foreign accent? Maria wanted to complete the interview before sunset. She feared that it was dangerous for any Latina to drive on country roads after dark among the descendants of Jefferson Davis.

As she drove up the dirt road to the Elly's farmhouse Maria was struck by the poverty that surrounded her. The road itself was scarred with potholes. The fences were badly in need of repair. Discarded farm machinery had been abandoned and left to rust. Many fields had not been cultivated in years; a mishmash of weeds was now the predominant crop. The barn and corncrib had not been painted in decades. Missing planks were everywhere, and unsecured doors flapped in the wind. The farmhouse was also in slow decay. Scattered chips of white paint still clung to a few pieces of siding, but most of the house was now shrouded in a dismal gray color. Several windows were boarded up and one of the gutters had fallen to the ground. The porch had separated from the house, leaving nearly a foot chasm for visitors to negotiate before entering.

Maria took a deep breath and carefully navigated the creaky porch steps. As she reached the top stair, she saw a pair of eyes peer through the curtains. How long had she been under surveillance? The front door swung open and a tall, gangly old man offered his hand to help bridge the gap between the house and the porch. Despite his frail appearance

Maria felt the strength in his arms as he helped her across the gap. The old man never spoke—not even after Maria thanked him for his help. He simply nodded, and gestured toward the diminutive woman who waited in the parlor. Mr. Elly then resumed his post, seated in front of the kitchen window with a shotgun lying across his lap and reading his bible.

Ethel Elly sat in a caned rocking chair which was draped in a black and gray afghan. She gestured to Maria to sit in an identical rocker. A small table with a brass lamp separated the two rockers. Motioning toward her husband, Mrs. Elly spoke first. "Don't mind him, miss. Oscar is harmless. He hasn't shot that old thing in twenty years, but the old fool insists on being prepared for Armageddon."

For the next four hours Maria listened to Mrs. Elly recount memories of her daughter while both women feasted on Ethel Elly's homemade blueberry muffins and lemongrass tea. Like many residents of the bootheel region, the Ellys were tenant farmers. Their primary crop was cotton. No matter how hard Ethel and Oscar Elly worked, they never could save enough money to buy their own land. They were devout Christians who belonged to a religious sect that combined fundamentalism with a rejection of all things modern including: electricity, gasoline powered machinery, and indoor plumbing. Mr. Elly cultivated his fields and picked his crops with horse drawn implements, and his wife cooked and heated their home with a wood burning stove.

Margo Elly did her homework from the dim light provided by a kerosene lamp. As a child she performed the usual chores assigned to farm children, milking their three cows and gathering eggs from their six hens. Her mother tried to teach her how to cook and bake, but Margo was much more interested in her books. She attended a one room school through eighth grade. Science was her favorite subject. Mrs. Elly remembered young Margo spending a lot of time in the woods watching animals in their natural habitat. In fifth grade she began conducting her own scientific investigations. In some early experiments she put different animal species (e.g. frogs and cats) in the same cage to see how they interacted with each other. In other projects she fed her animal subjects a variety of substances (including known poisons) to study their effects.

According to her mother Margo was never interested in dolls or playing house like most other girls. She could not remember any time when her only child engaged in imaginary play like pirates, cowboys and Indians, or doctor. Even as a child she was only interested in plants and animals that could be observed and physically manipulated. Young Margo had no childhood friends. She never invited any of her classmates to her home; nor was she ever asked to the homes of the other children. In high school she remained a recluse. She never joined any clubs, participated on athletic teams, or attended any high school dances. She was a straight A student and took all of the science and math courses available. Biology and chemistry were her favorite subjects. Mrs. Elly reported that her daughter had won many science contests and received numerous certificates, ribbons, and plaques.

Innocently, Maria asked, "Do you have newspaper clippings or other mementos of your daughter's accomplishments?"

"No. My husband felt that awards and prizes promoted the sin of pride. He made Margo burn all the awards while he recited a prayer thanking God for the gifts that He had bestowed on his daughter and asking Him to preserve her humility."

"How did your daughter feel about the destruction of her rewards?"

"Margo was hurt and angry, but she never complained. She knew that her father would give her his belt, if she uttered one word of protest."

"And how did you feel about your husband's approach to teaching humility to your daughter?"

"In those days I never questioned Oscar. Now I'm not so sure. Maybe, if we hadn't been so insistent on protecting her from the sin of pride, she would not have forsaken her religion and us. Margo never returned home after her second year in college; her letters stopped coming after her graduation. Some folks think that our strict ways drove her away. Maybe they are right," sadly sighed Mrs. Elly.

While Mrs. Elly was in the kitchen fetching more tea and muffins Maria scanned the parlor for family pictures. However, the room was barren of any images of Margo or her parents. When Mrs. Elly returned, Maria asked to borrow a photo of Margo that would accompany her story.

"I don't have any, dear. Our religion forbids photographs and portraits; they are considered sins of vanity."

"I'm sorry. I didn't know."

"No offense taken, Miss Flores. Even a strong believer like me questions that prohibition sometimes."

A tear rolled down Ethel Elly's cheek which she quickly wiped away. Maria's instinct was to reach across the table and gently touch the elderly woman on the arm, but her brain told her that this mother would be more upset than comforted by such a gesture. Emotional displays were undoubtedly discouraged by her ascetic religion. Maria rose from her rocking chair and thanked Mrs. Elly for her hospitality and taking the time to talk with her. As she stepped onto the porch, she nodded to Mr. Elly who continued to read his bible and guard his crumbling sanctuary from the evils of modernity.

The sun was setting as Maria left the Elly's farm. She made her way toward I-55 as quickly as possible. Her body was trembling. Her imagination ran amuck. She saw herself stranded on the shoulder of the highway, peering under the hood of her Japanese car as three rednecks straight out of the movie *Deliverance* approached her. She had no doubt that she was going to be raped and killed. Although Maria kept telling herself that she was being irrational, she still tried to make a perfect act of contrition to avoid going to hell for all of the mortal sins that she had committed with Graham. Her prayer was insincere, however; she was not truly sorry for those sins. Finally, she reached the interstate and her heart rate slowed slightly. Maria remained vigilant, however, constantly checking the rear view mirror for pick-up trucks adorned with the confederate flag. Not until she was ten miles from Delphi did she relax her guard.

CHAPTER 41:
GRAHAM HUNTER OCTOBER 28

Hunter had not seen Maria in several days which seemed like an eternity. He could not believe how dependent he had become on this flower from Chile. Tonight was the first time that he would be entertaining her at his home, and he was totally flustered. He was cooking the only gourmet dish in his culinary repertoire, chicken tarragon. The side dishes were fresh asparagus and risotto with saffron which Hunter was preparing for the first time. He had chosen a Spanish Rueda to complement the meal, or, if need be, mask any cooking errors. Maria was bringing a flan for dessert. Although Hunter had splashed significant amounts of Polo over his body after his shower, the aroma of garlic and tarragon now overwhelmed any sensual scent that he had hoped to transmit.

Graham's uneasiness was not solely a product of anxiety about his cooking for Maria. He also feared that his abode was furnished more like a museum than the home of an eligible bachelor. Not only did he live in the dirt and disorder typical of many single men, but he had changed little in the house since his mother's death. The living room was the biggest disaster. The fabric on all the chairs and sofa was worn and faded lace doilies adorned the armrests. The dark brocaded drapes were from another century and ladened with dust. The carpet was so dirty and worn that Hunter no longer knew if the original color had been beige or gray. The most suffocating aspect about this room was the lack of light.

The kitchen still had the same cabinets and countertops that were installed when the home was constructed in 1922. The stove and refrigerator were vintage 1950. The dining room was the best furnished room in the house. The dark mahogany furniture was well crafted and conveyed solid middle class values. A silver tea service graced the top of the sideboard. The flowered wallpaper and light fixture complemented the other furnishings. Graham decided to entertain Maria in this room as much as possible.

With the exception of his bedroom, Hunter had closed the doors on all of the rooms on the second floor. He hoped that Maria's curiosity would not force him to reveal the dust and clutter in these rooms. In anticipation of Maria's inaugural visit to his boudoir, he had bought new sheets and a comforter for his bed. He had even gone the extra mile and scrubbed the bathroom multiple times with Lysol. Plug-in air fresheners had been placed strategically around the house to conceal at least some of the odors of bachelorhood.

Graham had just finished the risotto when Maria arrived. Before sitting down for the meal, she insisted on a tour of the house. Contrary to Graham's worst fears, Maria found many of Mrs. Hunter's artifacts charming. Her only suggestion was to remove the heavy drapes and let in the sunlight. When the tour moved to the second floor she respected the closed doors and simply stated, "Graham, I am not afraid of dirt. So, when you decide to do some housecleaning and make a donation to Catholic Charities, I am more than willing to help." As she was escorted into Graham's bedroom she gave him a kiss and proclaimed, "I think that I could be comfortable in this room."

Pacabel's Canon in D major was playing when the couple returned to the dining room. Graham always thought of wedding processionals when he heard this music in which the same joyful theme is repeated with greater intensity and passion. The meal was perfect. Graham had even remembered to buy Maria's favorite brand of coffee, Kaldi's. Although she was quite impressed with her Yanquee's cooking acumen, she cringed when she saw the mess that he had made in the kitchen. She was not sure that she could ever allow Graham access to her kitchen regardless of how tasty the meal.

The dinner conversation had focused on Graham's parents. It was impossible to sit at Mrs. Hunter's dining room table without feeling her presence, and one could not reminisce about her without talking about her husband. After Maria served the flan, Graham shifted the conversation to her interview with Margo Elly's parents. They both were mystified by the complete estrangement between the deceased and her parents. They intellectually understood why the scientist could not submit to the fundamentalist religion of her parents, but to sever all communication with one's family was inconceivable for them.

Graham also solicited Maria's ideas regarding the murder investigation. Ever since she had resigned her position as the crime reporter for the *Scribe* their conversations had become much less guarded. Graham valued her insights regarding the possible motives of the suspects. He also thought that her investigation of Elly's background might reveal information relevant to solving the case. Graham was surprised at how analytical Maria was in her thought processes. Her logic was impeccable and she was comfortable going back and forth between inductive and deductive analyses of a problem. Graham had expected her to approach problems more instinctually, but she resorted to intuition much less than he did.

Maria's change in assignment at the *Scribe* had allowed her to become a partner with Graham in his investigation. She had immersed herself in the complicated hodgepodge of facts, speculations, and frustrations of the case. Graham no longer had to be careful about withholding information from her. Maria had not formed any clear opinion regarding Margo Elly's killer. She no longer thought Primal Man was too timid to be a killer; his messages and actions were getting increasingly more aggressive. She also wondered if his speech impediment was fueling his rage even more. She understood his pain at being forced to communicate his thoughts and feelings through index cards. It was a familiar pattern; the victim of maltreatment becomes a perpetrator of abuse.

Maria could not rationally exonerate Mike Hammer, but she still saw him as a victim rather than a potential murderer. She felt that Savage was capable of murder and his finger prints had been found at the scene of the crime. Jacob Spearman also had a personality that was easy for any thinking woman to despise, but she questioned whether he had sufficient nerve to kill Margo Elly. Nevertheless, Maria couldn't wait for the pornography arrest. Although she knew that Sally Heater was a casualty of some misguided notion of feminine beauty and style, she could not contain her laughter as Graham described her wardrobe, make-up, and coiffure.

Maria urged Graham to ignore the email evidence until the computer geeks completed their analysis. The autopsy report both fascinated and puzzled her. She found it intriguing that Elly was not brutally raped but rather literally scared to death. Such a finding did not seem consistent with her view of the deceased. She did not think that Margo Elly would frighten easily.

Having thoroughly reviewed all of the evidence Maria and Graham decided it was time for bed. However, the night ended without the usual sexual ecstasy that had been characteristic of their relationship. Despite his best intentions and a lot of gentle, and not-so-gentle, massaging by Maria, Graham could not perform. He did not want to admit it, but he feared that Maria was right. There were ghosts in the house. Graham had not totally escaped his Catholic background; he felt guilty having sex in his parents' home. Maria tried to reassure him that this was a temporary phenomenon; she reminded him that everything had functioned superbly in her apartment. However, Graham hated the idea of his libido being under the control of an over-active superego.

CHAPTER 42:
GRAHAM HUNTER OCTOBER 30

Maria had been on Graham's case about his eating habits, particularly his sugary breakfasts and his nightly snack of Cheetos. Consequently, the overweight detective was choking down a low fat blueberry yogurt when O'Rourke arrived for their morning briefing. The freckled faced cop had a box under his arm and a big grin on his face. Obviously, he had enjoyed serving the search warrant on Jacob Spearman.

"Dr. Spearman was more than a little annoyed about losing his video collection."

"Did he make the connection between our two visits?"

"Are you the puritanical pig investigating the demise of the Ice Queen? If so, Dr. Spearman's lawyer may be calling soon—something about police harassment."

"Well in that case we had better look at the evidence quickly."

Kevin and Graham sorted through the fifty or so tapes commenting on the titles: *Jugs and more Jugs, Deep Pussy,* and *Sword Swallower.* Based on the descriptions on the videos, none of the tapes seemed to violate community standards prohibiting child pornography or excessive violence. Two tapes, however, had hand written titles: *Sally Revealed* and the *Ice Queen.*

"Bingo!" exclaimed Graham. "Perhaps now we will truly see what excites our Dr. Spearman."

The first tape began with a strip tease by a reluctant Sally Heater with a lot of verbal encouragement from Director Spearman, including promises of the best purple bud she had ever smoked. Once Ms. Heater was totally revealed Spearman abandoned his position behind the camera, joining Ms. Heater on the plaid couch to bring this movie short to its climax.

The next tape proved far more interesting. Sally Heater once again was the leading lady. This time she was dressed in a white lab coat and wore a wig with straight black hair. Ms. Heater was even more reluctant to go before the camera for this drama.

She pleaded with Spearman. "Jake, this is too kinky! Why can't we just make love like normal people."

Spearman was insistent and reminded her of their earlier bargain, "No movie. No more cocaine, baby."

With that declaration Spearman left his station behind the camera and made his stage entrance. He was dressed as an executioner (black mask, tights, and boots). He carried a whip in his right hand and two pairs of hand-cuffs in his left. "Ice Queen, now you are in my power. Tonight I am giving you what you have wanted for all of these years. Strip!"

Awkwardly Sally Heater removed the lab coat and revealed her shapely body clad in a chain mail bra and thong. Then Spearman handcuffed her to a bookcase and cracked the whip. It did not touch Ms. Heater, but she was clearly afraid.

"Stop it, Jake. I don't want to play this game any more," pleaded Sally.

Spearman ignored her and proclaimed, "Ice Queen, now feel the sting of my shaft."

"Jake, please stop; you are scaring me," whined Sally.

Spearman snapped the whip again and exclaimed, "Taste the Prince of Darkness and you will be unfrozen."

"Holy shit!" exclaimed O'Rourke. "Dr. Spearman is one sick dude."

"Spearman is a real psycho, but the tapes are probably legal. Ms. Heater consented and there is no blood."

"How about the cocaine?"

"We actually never saw any cocaine, so we have no drug case. Fortunately we do have fresh evidence in the Margo Elly murder."

"How so?"

"'Ice Queen' is the derogatory nickname used to describe Margo Elly by faculty and students at Delphi. I think that it is time to bring in Dr. Spearman for a more formal interrogation to see if he acted on this fantasy and murdered the Ice Queen. However, we better seek the opinion of our distinguished county prosecutor before we arrest our porn star."

CHAPTER 43:
DONALD SPEAK OCTOBER 29

Once again Donald Speak turned to alcohol to relieve his anxiety—Bloody Mary's for breakfast, Manhattans with lunch, martinis before dinner, and scotch as needed. He had once been Sinduce's most trusted confidant, particularly with regard to how to handle the faculty and the media. Now she blamed her old friend for not being able to manage the crises that had descended on the Delphi campus. Speak's plan to dispatch Savage to Africa was on hold because of the Elly murder investigation. Similarly, he had been unable to silence Hilda German and the New Amazons. Sinduce had chastised him for not being able to control CNN and the other news organizations that continued to spew negative publicity about the campus. The president no longer began her day with a morning meeting and café latte with Speak. The VP of IT was now stirring the president's morning coffee.

His good friend, Liz Gold, had become an emotional wreck. Two years ago the president had hired her former classmate as her development director. Sinduce and Gold had been friends since attending St. Pristina the Virgin Martyr. Liz had been a successful consultant and fund raiser for the Democratic Party. Even during the Regan revolution she was able to get her candidates elected. Her skills, however, were no match for Newt Gringrich. None of her candidates could survive the "Contract *Against* America."

Despite her recent failures the president had been confident that her friend could successfully adopt her fund raising prowess to hustling money for the Museum of Medicine. Unfortunately the capital campaign had totally collapsed. Gold's push-up bras and cleavage revealing cocktail dresses had not raised a single dollar for the MOM. Prospective contributors refused to meet with her, and some donors had actually revoked their pledges of support. Now she rarely left her apartment. Depressed she sought refuge in food and TV. During the day she numbed herself with soap operas and binged on ho-ho's, ding dongs, and Edy's ice cream. Every night she self-medicated on Doritos, Fritos, Pringles, and old Doris Day movies. Instead of sleek designer clothes she now wore garments that looked more like tents. The once loquacious and over-exposed Liz Gold had become silent and invisible.

At first Speak had politely refused Gold's invitation to cohabitate with her, but finally he succumbed to her desperate plea. Now he sat in bed with his friend watching an old romantic comedy with Rock Hudson and Doris Day. He had finished half a bottle of scotch and Liz had consumed two large bags of Cheetos. Neither of them had been to campus in two weeks. Gold was resigned to being fired, but Speak was not giving up yet. He knew that their only hope for holding onto their jobs was to discredit ONO, the nickname that they had bestowed on Onan based on his initials. Speak had no doubt that he was a crook; he just had to prove it. Unable to sleep he left Gold to her addictions and hurried to the Oracle. He knew it was crazy, but he felt compelled to seek the wisdom of the sage. He patted the head of the young Roma child who offered to be his guide and gave her a dollar. He smiled graciously at the priestess and humbly entered the sanctuary. The sweet smell of lavender, followed by the putrid smell of rotten eggs, filled his nostrils. A stern voice greeted him,

"Counselor, what burden causes you to visit this old woman so late?"

"How can I save my job and that of my dear friend?"

"You must unmask the one who would take your place."

My God, thought Speak. The woman really is a soothsayer. She knows ONO is a fraud. Determined to make the Oracle's prophecy come true, Speak walked briskly to Gold's apartment. His friend was so engrossed in her misery and her addictions that she didn't even question Speak about his absence from her bed. She simply pecked him on the cheek and slid her hand down his leg hoping to arouse him and provide a temporary escape from their predicament. However, the booze would not permit Speak to rise to the occasion. He gently kissed his friend on the forehead, turned and faced the blank wall, and fell asleep with a sense of purpose that he had not experienced in months.

Early the next morning Speak sneaked into his office and logged into the university's accounting system. It took him only a few minutes to find the accounts controlled by VP Onan. It took another half hour for him to discover some unusual transfers. Quickly he drafted an anonymous letter for Detective Hunter and left the office. Speak's next stop was the office of the VP of IT. He had requested the meeting ostensibly for ONO to review the public relations announcements regarding Dr. Elly's patents and the Women in Science fund. He was kept waiting for nearly an hour. After gaining entry to Onan's inner office, he handed the VP the folder with the press releases. ONO quickly scanned the material and made a few minor corrections. Speak retrieved the folder and politely thanked Onan for his feedback. Safely back in his own office the communications director prepared another package for Detective Hunter.

CHAPTER 44:
GRAHAM HUNTER NOVEMBER 1

The county prosecutor took two days to study the Spearman videos. Hunter suspected that bible thumping Mather watched the tapes multiple times, probably alone and with his trousers around his ankles. However, when the prosecutor called Graham into his office he pontificated for ten minutes on the depravity of modern society and the need to expunge vermin like Spearman.

"What method of obliteration do you suggest, Justin—the rack or burning at the stake?"

"There you go again, Graham. Go ahead and laugh at the moral depravity that is consuming this country. Some day you will rot in hell for your complicity."

"If so, I will be in good company. The Supreme Court and those depraved souls that wrote the Constitution will be roasting with me."

"God, you are a wise ass. Let's go see Judge Solomon and see what she has to say."

Judge Solomon listened patiently to Mather rail against Spearman and the other pornographers of the world. In the end she agreed with Hunter that the video collection did not violate community standards and should be returned to him. However, she did order the police to retain the "Ice Queen" video as potential evidence in the Margo Elly case. She also agreed with the prosecutor's recommendation to issue an arrest warrant for Jacob Spearman.

"Hunter, I hope that this Spearman is our man. I can't tell you how many calls a day I get complaining about how slow and incompetent the criminal justice system is. We need a conviction soon."

"Sorry, Justin. I am as eager as you to solve this case, but we just don't have enough evidence against any of the suspects yet. We need to keep digging."

Hunter left a crimson red Mather steaming in front of the court house and went to arrest Spearman. Sally Heater was back at her usual station, but she had a new style, "Beatnick Greaser." Her platinum hair was still teased, and she was dressed entirely in black (tight fitting turtle neck, leather mini-skirt, thigh high boots, and matching beret). Her nails and lips were also painted black. As Graham waited for Ms. Heater to buzz him into Spearman's office, he couldn't help but speculate about what it must have cost him to retain his receptionist/ movie star. Hunter's return visit clearly annoyed Jacob Spearman.

"Now what is it, detective?"

"I am returning your video collection. Judge Solomon didn't like most of the movies—not enough plot. However, she did ask me to keep the 'Ice Queen' drama as potential evidence. Oh, and by the way, you are under arrest for the murder of Margo Elly. Anything that you say can be used against you. If you cannot afford an attorney, the state will provide one for you."

"Detective, I know it looks bad, but I didn't kill the bitch. I made that video over two years ago. I was in a bad way. It was two days after my son's sixth birthday. The prohibition against visiting my child has been the most painful thing I have endured in all my life. I regularly send him birthday and Christmas cards, but he never writes back. I suspect that my ex-wife intercepts all of my letters. The boy will be an adult before I can explain my absence; I fear it will be too late then. The video was therapy for me."

"Your little play certainly scared the pants off Ms. Heater. I wonder what a jury will think of it."

"Come on, detective. You need more evidence than that."

"We're working on it, Dr. Spearman. Do you want to call your attorney and tell him to meet us at the police station?"

Hunter enjoyed the irony in escorting a hand-cuffed Jacob Spearman passed an unshackled and relaxed Sally Heater. Maria Flores recorded the entire exit scene on her video camera. Spearman remained silent during the ride to the police station. Once inside his cell he flopped on the bed, turned his head toward the wall, and began pounding his fists into his mattress.

An hour later Spearman was interviewed by Hunter in the presence of his attorney.

"Dr. Spearman, where were you on the night Dr. Margo Elly was murdered?"

"Like I told you before, detective, I was at Club Erotica."

"The bartender does remember seeing you on the night of the murder, but he doesn't remember when you left. So the way I see it, you got your libido all worked up looking at a lot of naked women. However, when the girls at Club Erotica would not satisfy your perverted desires, you decided to pay a visit to your old nemesis, Dr. Elly."

"That's bullshit! And you know it."

Hunter kept pressing the frightened, but defiant, Spearman, "Tell me, Jake, did you intend to kill her or just scare the shit out of her?"

"Detective, I was not there. I was getting my rocks off at Club Erotica!"

"Unfortunately, Jake, nobody noticed what time you left the club, so you have no alibi."

Spearman's attorney interrupted at this point, "Excuse me detective. Most citizens of Delphi could not provide an alibi for their whereabouts on the night Dr. Elly was killed. Do you have any other evidence against my client?"

"In fact we do, counselor. We have a video made by your client that demonstrates quite graphically that he harbored murderous feelings toward Dr. Elly."

"No jury is going to convict my client of murder based on an old video."

"We also have a threatening email that your client sent Dr. Elly four days before she was killed."

"That email is bogus," shouted Spearman.

"You will have to prove that to the jury." Hunter's voice became more sympathetic, but the content of his interrogation became even more accusatory. "Jake, why don't you just come clean? I don't think that you have the balls to kill Dr. Elly. Here's what I think went down. You got sexually aroused at Club Erotica. Because of alcohol or some other substance, your frontal lobe got weak and you no longer could control your hate for Dr. Elly. Then you made a late night visit to teach her a lesson. Once inside her home you bound and gagged her like you had fantasized in the "Ice Queen" video. Then you began torturing her slowly. What did you do first—cut her breasts or beat her thighs

151

and buttocks with the miniature bat? Unfortunately, your performance was too convincing and Dr. Elly's heart too weak. And poof, you killed her. If that's what happened, Jake, the county prosecutor will cop a plea for second degree murder or maybe even manslaughter. However, if you don't confess, Jake, it's murder in the first degree (death or life imprisonment). Think about it."

"Detective, that scenario is total fiction. I am glad the bitch is dead, but I didn't kill her."

Spearman's lawyer intervened, "Detective, if this is all the evidence that you have, I can't wait to try this case. If you have no more questions for my client, I think that we should conclude this interview and you should release my client. You haven't got enough evidence to hold him."

"That is a decision for the court. I suggest that you make your case for bail with Judge Solomon. For the time being your client will remain a guest in my jail. Have a nice day!"

Hunter returned to his office and read the report from the FBI's computer expert regarding the emails that had been found on Margo Elly's computer.

> Dear Detective Hunter,
>
> We have traced the origins of the three email messages found on Dr. Margo Elly's computer. However, our analysis probably raises more questions than it answers. Let me explain in more detail. The email from Primal Man to Dr. Elly was sent from a student computer lab in the Murky Social Science Building, using a Yahoo account that had been opened on October 1. Jacob Spearman's alleged message was sent using a Hotmail account that had been opened on October 3. The email was sent from an internet café located near Dr. Spearman's home. It is certainly possible that the writers were Primal Man and Jacob Spearman. However, given that all of the correspondence originated from public access computers, we cannot establish beyond a reasonable doubt that any of the emails were in fact from the alleged senders. It is easy to establish both Yahoo and Hotmail accounts under any name; no identification is required. Because the accounts were

only used once, we could not determine if any other computers had accessed those accounts. Thus, it is certainly possible that some individual or individuals could have established the accounts for both Primal Man and Jacob Spearman for nefarious purposes.

The message from Dr. Savage did not originate from his office computer; it was sent from a computer in the Delphi University library. The sender did use Professor Savage's university account, so the sender had to know his account name and password. However, anyone familiar with Delphi University's computing procedures and Professor Savage could have made an educated guess about both the account name and the password. Alternatively Dr. Savage may have carelessly posted the password in his office somewhere; unfortunately, we see that a lot in academia. So, once again there is some ambiguity as to the author of this email. In conclusion, I am sorry that our analysis was unable to provide you with clearer evidence as to the originators of these emails.

At your request we also searched the back-up files that contained all of the email messages sent and received by Dr. Elly's computer for the past five years; back-up files were not available for any earlier time periods. We looked for messages sent by or sent to Primal Man, Jacob Spearman, and George Savage. There were no other communications between Dr. Elly and Primal Man other than those discussed in the previous paragraph. Five years ago the following message was sent from Dr. Elly to Dr. Spearman while he was still a university employee: "Resign or be crucified." Approximately one year later Dr. Spearman sent an email message from Jones Medical Supply to Dr. Elly that reads, "Hope that you are satisfied. I have lost my wife and child. Someday I will have my revenge." On October 3 of this year Dr. Elly sent the following message to Dr. Savage: "Abandon your fling with Emily, or you will be sorry!" No other communications between the victim and the three suspects were found.

Signed: Joseph Banks, Information Technology Division, Federal Bureau of Investigation

Once again Hunter rose from his chair, grabbed his therapeutic tennis ball, and began bouncing it off the walls in his office. Despite all the high tech analyses, the computer evidence was still ambiguous. Hunter's intuition told him that at least some of the emails were fake. One of the suspects was creating phony email evidence to throw suspicion on others. After thirty more minutes of tennis ball therapy and no new insights into Margo Elly's murder or the identity of Primal Man, Hunter decided to call it a day. For dinner Graham picked up two small salads from Wendy's. His resolve to eat better was not complete, however, as he smothered the lettuce with massive amounts of fatty bacon and ranch dressing. Classical trumpet music by Wynton Marsalis provided the background for his reanalysis of the information that he had received earlier in the day. The notes were clear, strong, and triumphant, but the music brought no new insights to the frustrated detective.

BOOK 4

REVELATIONS

The universe as we know it is a joint product of the observer and the observed. (Teilhard de Chardin)

Always recognize that human individuals are ends, and do not use them as means to your end. (Immanuel Kant)

CHAPTER 45:
PRIMAL MAN NOVEMBER 1

Normally the Delphi campus was bustling with activity until the library and the student union closed at midnight, but Primal Man had turned the campus into a ghost town after sunset. The women of Delphi University were clearly afraid to venture from their dorms with a sexual pervert lurking in the dark. A library or a student union sans women had little appeal to the Delphi men.

Primal Man had been invisible for over a week. The time had come for him to reappear. German and the New Amazons had burned his sacred texts, and the police had arrested his leader. They would pay a heavy price for their sins. For five days he had been watching the undercover cop strut her stuff on the dark, lonely road bordering the Olympic Forest. The hussy thought she could ensnare him by flaunting her tits and perfect legs, but he was no fool. He had seen her talking to the silver brooch on her blouse and adjusting the earpiece hidden behind her long blonde hair. He knew that she was not alone. A block away hidden behind a tall hedge he spotted the unmarked car manned by her male companion. On one occasion he had crept so close to the car that he could hear the freckled faced cop entertain the strumpet by singing Irish folk songs.

The young stalker had studied the movements of the bitch bait and her male shadow for three nights from a perch high in an old oak tree. Now he was ready to act. His prey was fifty feet away when he swooped down from his arboreal hideout. As the female cop approached him he thrust opened his rain coat and proudly displayed his manhood. She ran toward him, gun drawn, ordering him to halt and raise his hands. And then, whoosh! She fell into the branch covered pit that he had dug earlier in the day. He pounded his chest and released the roar of an angry ape. Quickly he dropped his card into the pit and sprinted into the Olympic Forest. He knew that her partner would soon be there to rescue her. Like all women she did need a man to protect her.

He was breathing hard when he reached the edge of the woods near his dorm. Before making his exit he changed from his uniform into civilian clothes. Gradually his heart and respiration rates returned to normal. Inside the safety of his room he savored his victory over the police. He could hardly wait to read the account of this battle in the *Scribe*. He knew the officers would not admit that they had been outsmarted by Primal Man, but the fact that he had escaped would make it clear to all of the residents of Delphi that he was indeed King of the Jungle. Soon they would stop harassing Professor Savage and the PMS. Then Primal Man could retire.

Gradually his exhilaration changed to sadness as it always did. He could never sustain the bold persona of Primal Man after he removed his vestments. In less than an hour he became a lonely college male again. He desperately wanted friends, particularly a girlfriend. He was not bad looking. His complexion was clear, and he had a good build. However, unless he was Primal Man, none of the co-eds noticed him. At least tonight he was not mute, but the animalistic scream that he had expelled scared him. It was not the person that he aspired to be. He wanted to be suave, not primitive.

The debate between the tenets of evolutionary psychology and Catholic dogma still consumed him. As Primal Man he was a soldier for Savage's PMS program. Once he removed Primal Man's war robe, though, he reverted back to the Catholic rituals of his boyhood. He had even started attending daily Mass. During the past week he had felt even more trapped and conflicted. Father Dominic had refused to absolve him of his sins after his attack against Professor German. According to the priest he must not be truly sorry for his sins against the women of Delphi because he continued his attacks. He did not want to go to hell, but who would stop German and the New Amazons if Primal Man vanished?

He also wondered if his little sister would be proud of him, or despise him, for his tactics against the radical feminists. He would never know, because he dared not talk to her about these issues; she was too young and innocent to understand biology and politics. He would have to decide between the Church and the PMS on his own. He clutched his rosary and prayed for guidance. Then he became feverish, perspired profusely, and shivered with the chills.

CHAPTER 46:
GRAHAM HUNTER NOVEMBER 2

Two mortified officers were waiting sheepishly in Hunter's office when he arrived shortly after midnight. Hunter's first concern was for O'Malley.

"Kathy, are you all right?"

"Only a sprained ankle and a few scratches."

"That's not what I meant. How are you emotionally?"

"Sir, I don't scare easily. I'm just embarrassed and angry."

"Don't be too hard on yourself. It could have happened to any one of us. Not often do suspects plan ahead and dig pits to capture police officers. Was there anything else special about this appearance of our friend?"

"Only one thing. When I was falling into the pit he pounded his chest and cut lose with an ape like howl."

"What was his message this time?" Hunter asked.

"'Stop harassing Professor Savage or else!'" read O'Malley.

"Kevin, do you have anything to add?" inquired Hunter.

"Only that I am sorry that we let you down, Graham."

"Kevin and Kathy, none of us are perfect. You need to stop apologizing and start strategizing. Any ideas?"

O'Malley spoke first. "Sir, I don't think we are going to capture this guy like we would a john who solicits prostitutes. He is not impulsive. He only strikes when he is ready. We need to find him when he is not wearing his Primal Man costume."

"What do you propose?"

"I think Kevin and I should spend a lot of time on campus, particularly in the PMS classes, looking for guys who have a speech impediment and are the same height and weight as Primal Man. There can't be that many. We can change our appearance enough by cutting and dying our hair. Kevin could even wear a fake beard; it would make him look more mature. I could don a pair of glasses to make myself look more intellectual."

"Kevin, what do you think?"

"It's worth a try. We certainly aren't making much progress hanging out by the woods."

"Okay, let's try Kathy's idea for a week. Now let's all go home and get some sleep."

After the two young officers left, Hunter breathed a sigh of relief. Thank God, O'Malley had not been seriously hurt, physically or emotionally. He was impressed with both her toughness and her analytical skills. Although it would take some time, her idea of looking for a male with a speech problem in the PMS classes seemed doable. He just hoped that they could identify the creep before he chose his next victim

CHAPTER 47:
MARIA FLORES, NOVEMBER 4

Maria Flores felt that her investigation of the life and death of Margo Elly was unfinished. Publication deadlines had forced her to go to print with two articles before she had finished her research. Even if another article was not forthcoming Maria wanted to interview Dr. Elly's former students, particularly Melissa Hope.

Dr. Hope cancelled two meetings with Maria before she finally relented. The interview had barely begun when Dr. Hope began sobbing uncontrollably. Maria gently touched her arm.

"I am sorry, Ms. Flores. I just don't know what to do."

"Maybe talking about it will help."

"I'm not sure. Things could get very ugly."

"I'm not following."

"Let me explain. I have information that could hurt Dr. Elly and Delphi University very badly. I begged Dr. Elly to do the right thing, but she wouldn't listen. Now she is dead."

"Can you tell me what this damning information is?"

"Ms. Flores, I failed to prevent a fraud. The research evidence that Dr. Elly submitted supporting the efficacy of Passion with Protection was incomplete. She failed to include the data on the negative side effects of the drug. I was the head research assistant on that project. You cannot imagine how many times I complained to Dr. Elly. I told her that we must report all of the data. Even after I graduated I kept badgering her but to no avail. At first I tried to appeal to her sense of ethics. A week before she died I finally summoned the courage to threaten her. I told her that if she did not submit the negative data, I would go to Smith Pharmaceutical and the FDA and reveal the truth. Dr Elly was furious, but she realized that I was serious. She told me that she wanted to think about her options; she promised to get back to me in a week. However, she was killed before she could give me her answer. Now I don't know what to do."

"What exactly is the problem with Passion with Protection?"

"The drug combines a spermicide to prevent pregnancy with testosterone to increase libido. The problem is with the dosage of the hormone—too little testosterone and there is no sexual arousal, but with too much testosterone our rats became overly aggressive. We had female rats that were so hyped up that they started acting like males and tried to mount their partners. In addition, some female rats on the drug became so aggressive that they seriously injured their partners during coitus."

"Did you experiment with the dosage?"

"We varied both the amount of the drug and the frequency of administration. We even tried to individualize the dosage level according to weight, age, and estrus cycle. Nothing we tried worked. I have never worked with a compound with such variable effects."

"I see your dilemma. What are you going to do?"

"I really have no choice now that Dr. Elly is dead. I am the only person who can make things right. I must contact Smith Pharmaceuticals and the FDA and keep the drug from coming to market. I have my old notebooks with the data on the negative side effects. This will mean that the Women in Science Fund will not receive any royalties from the Passion with Protection patent. I hate the idea of taking away scholarships from women who want to pursue science careers, but the drug is just too dangerous in its current formulation."

"Dr. Hope, thanks for sharing this with me. If it is any consolation, I know that you are doing the right thing. I only have one request. Would you object to me writing a story on this issue once you have had your discussions with the FDA? The article would focus more on your dilemma and your courage than the unethical behavior of Dr. Elly."

"Let me think about it. I never intended to hurt Delphi University or Dr. Elly. Right now I still feel more like a traitor than a hero."

"I understand. Let's keep in touch. Regardless of whether you consent to the story or not, I would like to know how this next chapter plays out. Best of luck."

CHAPTER 48:
GRAHAM HUNTER NOVEMBER 4

Hunter opened the door to his office and immediately spied an envelope on his desk with no return address. He did not even pour himself a cup of coffee before he ripped opened the envelope and found the following message: "If you want to catch the criminals of Delphi University, follow the money." Two cups of coffee and twenty minutes of tennis ball meditation produced no insight into the meaning of the anonymous letter. Frustrated Graham left the office for Father Dominic's. Dom greeted Graham with the usual bear hug and more coffee. After reading the message multiple times Dom asked, "Graham, what criminals are we talking about?"

"I haven't a clue. That's why I am here. It's hard to see how money could be involved in the Primal Man incidents. However, given Dr. Elly's patents perhaps there is a financial angle to her murder that we have not considered. Of course, the writer could be referring to some other crime that has not yet come to light. Finally, there is always the possibility that the informant doesn't know what the hell he or she is talking about."

"If I were looking for evidence of financial misconduct at the university, I would start in the offices of Liz Gold, Director of Development, and Owen Nigel Onan, Vice President of Innovative Technology. Gold has responsibility for raising money for the university from traditional donors. Onan was hired to increase revenues for the university through partnerships with industry. He also is the one who will oversee the disbursal of the revenue generated by Dr. Elly's patents."

"Based on Onan's performance at Margo Elly's funeral, I suspect that he is quite capable of engaging in creative accounting and other petty crimes to further his own personal goals. Perhaps he is even capable of murder for the right price?"

"Graham, Gold is also desperate. I think that she would sell her body, and perhaps even her soul, for a large donation to the Delphi University Development Fund. President Sinduce has made it clear that she will be fired by the end of the year if she does not raise ten million for her legacy building, the Museum of Medicine."

"Dom, I don't want to alert either Gold or Onan that they are under suspicion. Is there a less intrusive way that we can follow the money?"

"I may be able to help. Our Catholic Student Association has an account at the university, so I have access to the university accounting system to track our expenditures and revenue. With a little help from a friend in the accounting department, I may be able to track the flow of money in the offices of both Onan and Gold."

Graham couldn't wait to tell Maria about the anonymous letter. She had agreed to make her famous empanadas, if Graham brought the wine. He had chosen an Argentine malbec, but as he rang Maria's doorbell he worried that a cabernet from Chile might have been a safer choice. Maria reassured him that she liked a number of Argentine creations including Gardel, Che Guevara, and malbec. Scheherazade by Rimsky-Korsakov provided the background music for the meal. The music was both mysterious and romantic.

The empanadas tasted like no meat pie that Graham had ever eaten; in addition to beef, his palate recognized cumin, eggs, olives, and raisins. Maria listened quietly, but intently, as Graham told his tale of the anonymous letter and Father Dominic's speculations on where the university money trail might lead. She then informed Graham of her meeting with Melissa Hope. Simultaneously both of them shouted, "Onan."

"Graham, I bet Margo Elly got scared when Melissa Hope threatened to expose her research misconduct. She probably told Onan that the university had no alternative but to cancel the patent agreement."

"The VP of IT would not like that news. I suspect that he had big plans for that revenue stream."

"I have no doubt that Onan is a thief, but do you think that he is a murderer?"

"Based on his crass eulogy for Dr. Elly, I think that he would commit any crime to foster his own self-interest."

"What are you going to do?"

"I need to determine if there was any financial misconduct being perpetrated by Gold or Onan. It would also be nice to know if Margo Elly had a meeting with Onan shortly before her death."

"Can't you just check the calendar on her computer?"

"Her research assistant told me that she did not use the computer to keep her appointments. She apparently used an old fashion appointment book, but we were never able to find it."

"Graham, I bet the high-tech VP of IT, or more likely his secretary, keeps an electronic calendar. Let me see if I can use my investigative journalism skills to find out if Onan and Elly had a meeting. Anything else?"

"What's for dessert?"

"No dessert for you until you lose five pounds, big boy. However, if you don't complain too much, I will give you a strenuous workout."

CHAPTER 49:
MIKE HAMMER NOVEMBER 5

After being released from jail Mike Hammer had moved into a cheap motel. It took him a month before he was ready to move back into the house that he had shared with his wife. He had hoped never again to step into the haunted dwelling that had caused him so much grief. He desperately wanted to flee Delphi. However, his realtor told him that he would have great difficulty selling the house until the hysteria surrounding the murder had dissipated. Even Hammer's coworkers at Walmart treated him differently now. Most avoided him; the few that offered their condolences with their tongues accused him of murdering his wife with their eyes. The Youth Soccer League would no longer let him coach the children of Delphi. The maxim of "innocent until proven guilty" did not apply to Mike Hammer. Most Delphi citizens were convinced that he was a sexual pervert and a murderer.

Mike Hammer started doubting his own innocence. Margo had certainly given him plenty of reason to hate her. Perhaps he had killed her during one of his drunken binges. He could not decide whether he should seek psychiatric help, or confess his guilt to Detective Hunter? In the end Mike Hammer did nothing. He kept as low a profile at Walmart as possible. He always ate his lunch alone and went for a solitary walk during his breaks. When the work day was through, he escaped to his den and sat in front of the TV until he fell asleep. Not even his dirty magazines excited him any more. Mike Hammer was spiritually and emotionally comatose. Not once had the abandoned husband summoned enough courage to enter his wife's bedroom or the living room which had been her exclusive territory. There certainly was no need to venture into the sadomasochism chamber now that Margo was gone.

CHAPTER 50:
DOMINIC ALONGI NOVEMBER 6

Gloria Lombardi, Father Dominic's mole in the accounting office, reported virtually no activity in any of Gold's accounts since the Primal Man incidents had begun. She had not been able to raise a single dollar in over eleven months. The accounts controlled by Onan on the other hand had been quite active. The day after Dr. Elly's death $100,000 from the Women in Science Fund had been transferred into the general operating account of the IT department to pay for office furniture. Lombardi also noticed that three recently appointed members of the Board of Curators had donated $10,000 each to the "IT Discretionary Fund."

"Gloria, why would these donors contribute money to Onan's discretionary account," Father Dominic asked?

"I don't know, Father, but I will keep digging. There has to be a reason other than simple philanthropy."

Dom left Lombardi to continue her forensic accounting. He had no doubt that Onan and his fellow conspirators were up to no good, but he decided to wait for a more complete picture of the crime before bothering Hunter. He also wanted to delay his meeting with Graham because of another problem. He now knew the identity of Primal Man, but he could not reveal his name because he had obtained this information during the sacrament of penance. He could not break the seal of confession; it was a sacred vow. He had recognized the young man from his stutter. He told him that he could not grant him absolution until he truly repented from his actions and ceased being Primal Man. The penitent remained silent for a few minutes and then exited the confessional without even reciting the Act of Contrition.

CHAPTER 51:
MARIA FLORES NOVEMBER 7

Maria had been mulling over her interview with Melissa Hope for several days. Something didn't fit. Why had Hope waited so long to confront Dr. Elly about her research misconduct? Was something else besides an ethical dilemma motivating her?

Maria decided to seek more information from Judy Lacky. Hope had been head research assistant before turning over that role to Lacky. Maria began her interview by asking about Elly's patent research.

"Ms. Lacky, how involved were you in the research on Spermicide Complete and Passion with Protection?"

"All of the research on those products was done before my time."

"Did you hear any gossip about possible negative side effects associated with either of these products?"

"No, what's this about?"

"One of Dr. Elly's former assistants, Melissa Hope, is alleging that Dr. Elly failed to disclose serious side effects associated with Passion with Protection."

"Oh, my God! What is she going to do?"

"It appears that she is going to take her charge to the FDA and Smith Pharmaceutical."

"How ironic!"

"What do you mean?"

"Ms. Flores, Melissa was Dr. Elly's pet. They went out together for dinner and drinks quite often. They even stayed in the same hotel room when they went to conventions. None of the rest of us had such a close relationship with Dr. Elly."

"I don't mean to pry, but do you think that Dr. Elly and Dr. Hope had a romantic relationship?"

"I never considered it before, but now I am not so sure."

"Did you ever hear of any recent friction between Dr. Elly and Dr. Hope?"

"No, but I have not seen or heard anything about Melissa in years."

Maria thanked the young research assistant and left the building. As she strolled through the campus, she reflected on Judy Lacky's revelation about the relationship between Margo Elly and Melissa Hope. Could they have been lovers? If so, had Elly rejected her for someone else? Would such a rejection have driven Hope to kill her former lover? Such speculations seemed far fetched, but Maria could not get them out of her mind. Unfortunately, she could not think of any easy way to ascertain the full extent of the relationship between the two women.

Maria then made her way to Onan's office. His secretary was more than willing to examine the calendar of the VP of IT after Maria claimed to be from the police department. While she waited for the secretary to complete her search, Maria gazed around Onan's office. The place was furnished with sleek black leather designer chairs, glass tables, oriental rugs, expensive artwork, Belgian chocolates, and Cuban cigars. The secretary interrupted Maria's visual surveillance to report that no scheduled meeting between Onan and Elly appeared on the calendar. Maria thanked her and left for home.

Cooking for Graham provided Maria a temporary respite from worrying about Melissa Hope. For no apparent reason she hummed the Chilean national anthem as she prepared a low calorie meal of roasted vegetables and rosemary chicken. Hayden's Concerto in E flat major for trumpet provided the mood music for the dinner. As they were having coffee sans dessert, Maria informed Graham that no scheduled meeting had taken place between Elly and Onan. She then provided Graham with a detailed description of Onan's office.

"I wonder how the VP of IT paid for his new office furnishings. I wouldn't be surprised if he raided the Women in Science Fund. Father Dominic's forensic accounting should be able to detect any larceny by Onan. However, given that we have no record of a meeting between Elly and Onan, let alone any conflict, nothing implicates him in Elly's murder."

"Graham maybe Onan realized that he could not steal from the Women in Science Fund while Elly was alive, because she would be too vigilant. After she was dead, however, he would have no problem skimming money from the fund as long as he awarded some scholarships each year."

"I will concede that point for the moment, but it's still hard to believe that the deceased would let Onan into her home at night?"

"Why not? They had never had a confrontation. Perhaps he called and asked to meet with her regarding ideas he had about promoting the Women and Science Fund. He might even have brought a bottle of wine to help relax her guard."

"But, why would he stage a rape?"

"The 'rape as ruse' theory applies to Onan just as it does to Savage and Spearman. The murderer stages a rape to throw the police off the track from his true motive."

"I can't deny your logic, but somehow it just doesn't feel right."

"Okay, Mr. Skeptical. Let me suggest another suspect, Melissa Hope."

"What do you mean? I thought she was just a whistle blower doing the ethical thing?"

"Apparently Dr. Elly and Dr. Hope had an unusually close relationship including going out for drinks and sharing a room at conventions. Dr. Elly did not have this type of relationship with any of her other students. For the sake of argument let's say that they were lovers at one time. What might happen if Dr. Elly found someone else and threw Dr. Hope overboard?"

"Christ, Maria, you are not helping! We need to eliminate suspects, not add them."

"Sorry, boss. Maybe we should call it a night. Perhaps our brains will work better in the morning after we exercise our bodies."

CHAPTER 52:
DOMINIC ALONGI NOVEMBER 8

Gloria Lombardi was extremely upset when Father Dominic walked into her office. "The president is going to sell the Olympic Forest to the Trojan Lead Company," she screamed.

"Didn't the board vote 7-2 against that sale just last month?"

"Yes, but Sinduce just replaced three board members with new appointees. All the outgoing members opposed the sale, but the three new ones voted in favor of it yesterday. Thus, the motion to approve the sale passed 5-4."

"Now Sinduce will have the money needed to build her Museum of Medicine."

"That's not the biggest problem, Father. Trojan Lead will destroy the forest to mine the lead below. Not only will we lose our beautiful forest, but the landscape will be scared, the rivers will become polluted, and lead dust will poison our children."

"Gloria, keep digging. These new board members must have received something in exchange for their votes."

Father Dominic hesitated to inform Hunter of Onan's plot until he had more details. However, he did have some good news regarding Primal Man. The flasher had returned to his confessional seeking forgiveness. Dom had prepared a personalized homily for the young man. He told him that God did not approve of the gender war that was taking place on campus. He reminded the young man that God had created both men and women in His image. Consequently, when he exposed himself to women, he was actually assaulting God. He told him that evolutionary psychology had no scientific merit and that Professor Savage was a charlatan. To his surprise the young man had not bolted from the confessional; nor had he tried to defend Savage. Without stuttering he had simply asked the priest what he must do to receive absolution and return to a state of grace. Father Dominic told him to cease being Primal Man, make a public apology to the women of Delphi, and go to counseling to better understand his feelings toward women. Calmly the penitent promised to do all of the things requested by the priest. Then he bowed his head and reverently recited the Act of Contrition.

Father Dominic couldn't wait to share the good news with Hunter. He brought pastry from the family bakery to celebrate the death of Primal Man with his friend.

"Dom, what brings you to this dismal place on a beautiful afternoon?"

"Jelly donuts for my best friend."

"Thanks, Dom, but I'm on a diet."

"Are you sick, or in love?"

"No comment."

"So, you are in love. I've noticed a certain swagger in your step and a gleam in your eye recently. Who is the lucky girl?"

"Can you keep a secret?"

"I will pretend that I heard this good news as your confessor."

"The mystery woman is Maria Flores."

"Mama Mia! You are a lucky boy. Not only is she gorgeous, but she is bright. When did you plan on introducing her to your best friend and religious counselor?"

"Soon, I promise. Dom, it scares the shit out of me, but I think this is the real thing,"

"Graham, I couldn't be happier for you."

"Enough about my love life. What really brought you to this hovel?"

"I bring you good news. Primal Man is dead."

"What do you mean?"

"The immature adolescent who assumed that identity confessed his sin to me this morning. Tomorrow, he will become a man. He is sending a letter of public apology to the women of Delphi that will appear in the *Scribe*."

"What about the criminal charges against him?"

"I can't help you there. The seal of confession prevents me from revealing his name."

"Jesus Christ, Dom! The little twerp has terrorized an entire community for two months, and his punishment is a letter of apology!"

"Believe me, this young man has learned his lesson. His guilt will be with him for a long time."

"Have you forgotten? Primal Man is also a murder suspect."

"Trust me. This young man is not capable of murder."

"Isn't that a decision for the criminal justice system to make rather than the Church?" responded Graham angrily.

"Sorry, Graham. I am not revealing the boy's identity."

"Dom, this does not make me happy. I know how important your vows are, but I no longer have faith in your Church or its customs. I hope to God that your instincts are correct and this boy is not a killer."

The elation that Father Dominic felt when he had entered Hunter's office quickly dissipated when he realized that his friend was not satisfied with Primal Man's retirement. He wanted the misguided boy punished. Dom understood his friend's point of view, but he did not share it. He was a priest, not a cop. Father Dominic planned to use Primal Man's apology as the first step in ending the gender war. He desperately wanted to heal the wounds that had been inflicted during the battles between the New Amazons and Darwin's Disciples. He hoped that Hilda German and George Savage would join him in publicly calling for an end to the conflict. He prayed for guidance, but his invocation lacked conviction. No divine intervention would be forthcoming. He was on his own.

CHAPTER 53:
GRAHAM HUNTER NOVEMBER 11

Hunter was so upset about the lack of progress in the Elly murder investigation that he went off his diet and bought two sausage and egg biscuits from Hardees. He had many suspects, but insufficient evidence to indict any of them. Seeking an escape from the quagmire Hunter decided to review all of the evidence in the case. He began with the autopsy report. After reading it for the third time, he shouted, "Eureka," and ran down the corridor to the medical examiner's office.

"Doc, sorry for the interruption, but I have to ask you about the Elly autopsy."

"Fire away, Graham."

"Your report suggested that Margo Elly died of myocardial infarction triggered by cardiac arrhythmia. Correct?"

"That's right, but I can't prove it."

"What would bring on such a cardiac event in a patient with no history of arrhythmia?"

"My hypothesis is that Dr. Elly became extremely frightened as she was being tortured. In response her adrenal glands secreted large amounts of epinephrine which increased her heart rate and blood pressure leading to cardiac arrhythmia and ultimately a heart attack."

"Isn't epinephrine also sold commercially?"

"Yes, it is widely available. EMTs sometimes administer it along with CPR to jump start the heart. It is also used to interrupt severe asthma attacks and to combat serious allergic reactions."

"What would happen if someone were intentionally given too large a dose of epinephrine?"

"Same result as if the adrenal glands had secreted the epinephrine—death triggered by cardiac arrhythmia."

"Would an autopsy be able to tell if the epinephrine in a person's body was secreted by the adrenal glands or administered externally?"

"Not usually. Because epinephrine is produced naturally by the body, toxicology reports cannot distinguish between an external administration of the hormone from an excessive supply produced naturally by the body. If the epinephrine were administered with a syringe, you might find traces of the drug at the injection site. Epinephrine can also be administered orally or through an inhaler, but it would be more difficult for a killer to administer an overdose using either of these methods because they would need some minimal cooperation by the victim. Graham, maybe we should request permission to exhume the body."

"Doc, what good would that do? Even, if we found an injection site and traces of epinephrine, we still have no evidence implicating a specific suspect. We need to find a syringe or an inhaler with finger prints. At the very least I want to find out if any of our suspects had access to epinephrine. I'll ask O'Rourke to tackle that part of the investigation."

Until O'Rourke finished his inquires there was nothing Graham could do on the Elly case. Still angry about Primal Man's escape from justice he decided to try his luck at finding a speech impaired flasher hidden among three thousand males on a five hundred acre campus. He began his search by wandering from group to group of students who were milling about the central quadrangle. It soon dawned on him that most speech impaired students probably did more listening than talking. His only chance of inducing the flasher to manifest himself was to engage male students of the same height and weight as the flasher in conversation. Thus, for the next four hours Hunter traveled from building to building asking directions to the library from every male who fit that description. In all that time he did not meet one speech impaired male, but he did learn how to get to the library from every possible location on campus.

Hunter needed to rest. His feet were cramping and his lower back ached. A bench in front of Poisedon's Pond promised respite. Graham slowly removed his shoes and stretched out on the bench. For the first time that day he took notice of the trees that were ubiquitous on campus. Nearly all of the fall foliage was gone with the exception of a few stubborn leaves of burgundy, crimson, and ocher that clung to the tree branches. The fatigued detective sighed. He had missed nearly the entire fall display of color, because he had been so engrossed in his work. How sad and unnatural!

DELPHI SCRIBE: LETTER TO THE EDITOR

November 11
Primal Man Repents

Dear women of Delphi,

For the past three months I assumed the identity of "Primal Man" in a misguided attempt to frighten you. After some serious soul searching, confession, and several conversations with Father Dominic Alongi, I now know that my actions were wrong. Primal Man will never frighten anyone again. Nothing that I can say in this letter can undo the harm that I have done. Nevertheless, I want the women that I threatened to know that I am ashamed of my actions and I am sincerely sorry for any psychological harm that I may have caused. I also apologize to all of the women of Delphi for creating an atmosphere of fear on campus. I especially regret my contribution to the hostility between male and female students that has surfaced on campus. I now repudiate all of the tenets of Professor Savage and the other evolutionary biologists who argue for biologically determined roles for men and women.

Signed: Primal Man in Recovery

Editor's note: The Delphi Scribe received the above letter yesterday. The writer indicated that Father Dominic Alongi, spiritual advisor to the Catholic students of Delphi University, could verify the veracity of the letter. Without revealing the identity of the letter writer Father Alongi confirmed the letter's authenticity. Now that "Primal Man" no longer exists, we sincerely hope that the women of Delphi University will once again feel safe on their campus. We also urge the New Amazons and Darwin's Disciples to declare an end to the war between the sexes that has plagued Delphi University during the past year.

CHAPTER 54:
DOMINIC ALONGI NOVEMBER 11

Father Dominic stood alone behind the lectern in the Delphi University auditorium as students and faculty quietly took their seats. Hilda German and George Savage had refused to join him on the stage. Savage called the priest a naïve sissy and rejected his proposal with an angry barrage of platitudes about biological destiny. German was more sympathetic, but she felt that she could not ask her supporters to declare a truce as long as the PMS program existed. Dominic would have to persuade the combatants to end their war without the support of their generals. His only consolation was that the New Amazons were not carrying their signs or chanting their anti-Savage slogan; German must have convinced her army that the priest was not their enemy.

Father Dominic took a deep breath and began. "Students and faculty, I bring you good news. Primal Man no longer exists. The young man who frightened the women of this community by exposing himself and leaving threatening messages has realized the error of his ways. He has written a formal apology to all of the women of Delphi that appears in today's edition of the *Scribe*. I hope that all of you will read this young man's letter and let it be the springboard for a new beginning for our campus. I urge you to join me in ending the gender war that has plagued our community. God did not create man and woman to be enemies. His plan was for men and women to help each other in their daily struggles on this beautiful planet we call earth.

Men, the advocates of the PMS program are false prophets. God did not rigidly proscribe specific roles for each gender that should remain invariant for all times. Women have a right to compete with you in school and in all occupations. You should not fear this competition. You should welcome it. The modern day work place is going to be much more interesting with more women working side by side with you. In addition, the changes in society that have come about because of the Women's Movement have some benefits for you. It is no longer taboo for a man to cry or to want to stay home and take care of his children. Men, you have many more options in life than your fathers. Don't be frighten by these choices; embrace them.

Women, the PMS program and Primal Man have treated you unfairly. Not all Delphi men are your enemies, however. You need to give your brothers another chance. If they offend you with outdated, chauvinistic ideas, don't reject them. Educate them! It is not easy for any of us to shed old ideas that were handed down to us by our parents and our teachers. It takes time to incorporate new ways of thinking into our daily lives. Please give the young men on this campus an opportunity to be your companions in life rather than your enemies.

Faculty, during this unsavory war too many of us sat silently on the sidelines. Academic freedom does not mean that we blindly accept every crazy idea that one of our colleagues puts forward. No, academic freedom requires that we speak out against those ideas that we consider erroneous or dangerous. Although most of us reject evolutionary psychology and sociobiology, none of us challenged these false beliefs in rational debate. We remained silent. No wonder Professor German and the New Amazons felt that they had no choice but to wage war. My fellow faculty members, we must never let this happen again. We cannot let the battle for the minds of our students remain solely in the hands of the extremists. We must speak out.

In closing I ask each of you to cast off the fear and anger that has enveloped us these past weeks. Ask forgiveness of each other and start a dialogue. These will be difficult conversations. You will not all come to the same vision of the world. It is okay to despise someone's ideas, but try not to hate the person who promulgates views with which you disagree. Remember God's most important commandment: Love thy neighbor as thy self."

As the priest stepped back from the podium, scattered applause rose from the audience. Several faculty members rose from their seats and shouted, "Bravo." Then the entire audience rose in unison and gave a thunderous ovation. Smiles and embraces erupted throughout the auditorium. Father Dominic had no idea whether the warriors were ready to sign an armistice, but he knew that the civilians would no longer support the war. His message had been heard.

Exhausted, but satisfied, the priest made his way to Gloria Lombardi's office. He still had another battle to fight. Lombardi was both excited and furious as she greeted Dom.

"Father, I now know why the new board members contributed money to Onan's slush fund. Each of them received no-bid contracts with the university."

"How is that possible, Gloria? I thought the university required bids on all its contracts."

"Although Delphi University rarely awards contracts without competitive bids, university regulations do permit no-bid contracts for less than $100,000 under special circumstances. I have no idea what justification was used, but Sinduce did approve no-bid contracts of $99,000 for each of the new board members."

"What services are these contractors providing the university?"

"Father, that's the issue that makes me the angriest. One board member is providing copying services for the university. Another has the contract for all the vending machines on campus. The third member is providing linen service for the campus. In the past we required sealed bids before awarding contracts for all these services. All three new vendors are charging more for the service than our previous providers."

"Gloria, the level of corruption of this gang of thieves is too much."

"It gets worse. All three board members and Onan recently bought stock in Trojan Lead."

"How did you find this out?"

"There is only one brokerage house in town, and my brother works there. When I told him the situation, he was more than willing to break client confidentiality."

"I have no doubt that VP Onan was the one who convinced President Sinduce to award these contracts and appoint these new board members. Sinduce gets her legacy building; Onan and the board members watch the value of their stock in Trojan Lead increase as they profit from shady contracts."

"This is not right. We have to do something."

"I will share this information with Detective Hunter. Maybe he can think of a solution."

CHAPTER 55:
HILDA GERMAN NOVEMBER 11

Hilda German had listened patiently to Father Dominic's plea to join him in declaring an end to the gender war. She knew the priest was right. Things had gotten out of hand. Some of her young supporters had wanted to arm themselves with guns. Others wanted to kidnap the children of the PMS professors, refusing to release them until the faculty member agreed to stop teaching in the program. In the end General German could not bring herself to join the priest and publicly renounce the war that she had begun. Such an appearance would have been a blatant admission that she had been wrong. She did, however, manage to sneak into the auditorium and hear the priest's speech. No one had noticed her sitting in the back row wearing a false mustache and a baseball cap. She could never admit it to the New Amazons, but she was pleased that the priest's message had been so well received. She too was tired of the war.

Exhausted Hilda German collapsed into her favorite recliner and raised the foot rest; her feet were aching. The demands of her role as leader of the New Amazons had exacerbated her health problems. Good nutrition had never been a habit practiced by German, but the stress of the gender war had made her nearly anorexic. Her constant anger fueled her high blood pressure. German sought relief from her foot pain by soaking her feet in a large pan of warm water laced with Epsom salts. As her aches dissipated Hilda reviewed her successes as general of the New Amazons. Primal Man had retired. Although the PMS sill existed on paper, her army had defanged the program. Its leader was a virtual prisoner in his home and accused of murder. She wished that she could have convinced George Savage, Jacob Spearman, and the other chauvinists that it was wrong to sleep with one's students, but these misogynists lacked any insight into how their actions affected others. Eventually the persona of General German gave way to her other self, teacher of literature. She longed for her former life when all her energy went into analyzing the novels of the Bronte sisters and Jane Austen. She was constantly amazed by the ability of these women to generate sentences that conveyed feelings, motives, and thoughts which were unique and consistent for each character over some three hundred pages or more. It was an incredible talent that she both admired and envied.

CHAPTER 56:
GRAHAM HUNTER NOVEMBER 12

Graham struggled to swallow the low-fat strawberry yogurt that Maria had substituted for his preferred breakfast of sugar and/or fat. He was under orders to lose ten pounds or return to celibacy. Graham's penance was interrupted by a knock on his door. He greeted his visitor, Father Dominic, with sarcasm.

"What brings you out so early? Shouldn't you be hearing the confessions of criminals?"

"Still angry about Primal Man, I see."

"Sorry, Dom. I know that I should be thanking you for persuading our exhibitionist to stop terrorizing the women of Delphi. But, I still don't like the idea of him escaping with an apology. Neither does Justin Mather."

"Perhaps my morning visit will get me back into your good graces."

"What do you have?"

"We have finished following the money. Gold is clean, but Onan and his gang are going to destroy the campus because of their greed."

The priest then detailed the information that Gloria Lombardi had found: Onan's raiding of the Women in Science Fund, the no-bid contracts, the contributions to Onan's slush fund, the proposed sale of the Olympic Forest to Trojan Lead, and the purchases of Trojan Lead stock by the conspirators.

"Holy shit, Dom! That's awful. Those bastards are willing to destroy the beauty of the campus and expose their fellow citizens to poison for a few bucks. Hanging is not a severe enough punishment for creeps like them."

"I agree, but how are you going to prove that they are guilty? My guess is that all these arrangements were made with a simple handshake."

"You are probably right, padre. If we can't produce enough evidence to indict them, perhaps Maria can expose their chicanery in the *Scribe*. Somehow this evil has to be stopped."

"Good luck, my friend. Now, I must return to my regular job."

Hunter was both upset and intrigued by Father Dominic's revelations regarding the planned sale of the Olympic Forest to the Trojan Lead Company. Like many residents of Delphi he spent hours roaming through the woods smelling and gazing at the topography and diverse flora and fauna that inhabited the forest. Graham was convinced that a crime had been committed, but without a paper trail he knew that a conviction was impossible. Moreover, he had no concrete evidence that the crimes being perpetrated by Onan and Sinduce were related to Margo Elly's death. Tennis ball therapy was not helping Hunter or the walls in his office when his meditation was interrupted by an angry Justin Mather.

"Graham, when the hell are you going to arrest someone for the murder of Dr. Elly? It has been over a month now. The media are crucifying the criminal justice system for its incompetence."

"Well, Justin, prepare yourself for more pain, because things are going to get worse."

"What's that suppose to mean, smart ass?"

"I have two more suspects in the Elly case, but not enough evidence to arrest either of them for murder. The Vice President of Innovative Technology, Owen Nigel Onan, appears to have been siphoning money from Elly's scholarship fund for his own purposes. Melissa Hope, a former student of Dr. Elly, threatened the professor with academic fraud. Unfortunately, we cannot place either suspect at the murder scene."

"My God, Graham, stop finding more suspects. Just nail one of them for the crime."

"I wish it were that simple, Mr. Prosecutor."

"Do you have any more good news for me, Graham, before I go and slit my throat?"

"In fact I do. It appears that there has been even more financial hanky-panky at Delphi University. The new Board of Curators just approved the sale of the Olympic Forest to Trojan Lead."

"My God, Graham! Those assholes are the worst polluters on earth. Why did the university agree to the sale?"

"President Sinduce needs the money to build her Museum of Medicine."

"Do you think a crime was committed?"

"Sure, but unless one of the conspirators decides to testify for the prosecution, I don't see how we can prove anything. I would be shocked if there were any documents detailing their treachery. However, I am sure that Maria Flores will be interested in the story. The press has much less burden of proof than we do."

"Graham, normally I regard the press as our enemy, but in this case they may do us some good. Go ahead and talk to Flores, but the next time I see you I want to hear that you have charged someone for Elly's murder."

"Justin, go back to your office, and stay away from sharp objects," chided Hunter dismissively.

The crimson faced prosecutor had the last word as he slammed the door, "Solve this case soon, Hunter, or we both will have to find new careers."

It took Hunter nearly an hour to calm himself after Mather left his office. Kevin O'Rourke's appearance provided a needed diversion. He had found out that all of the suspects, with the possible exception of the mysterious Primal Man, had access to epinephrine. Onan was severely allergic to poison ivy and a number of other plants, so he was never without his preloaded syringes. George Savage carried an inhaler containing epinephrine with him at all times because of his asthma. Jacob Spearman had access to the drug through his connections as a distributor of medical supplies. Melissa Hope used the substance in her research. Mike Hammer had access through his wife. Margo Elly was extremely allergic to bee stings; she carried an inhaler with her at all times. She had taught Hammer how to use an epipen in case she ever became incapacitated because of a sting.

Hunter was still trying to absorb all of the information that Dom and Kevin had dumped on him in the previous two hours when the afternoon mail was delivered. His eyes were immediately drawn to another letter with no return address. Inside were two press releases from Delphi University. A note claimed that VP Onan had left his finger prints on the documents. The writer suggested that Hunter run the prints through the FBI finger print file. He was convinced that a match would be found. The author admitted that he had no idea if Onan was his real name, but he had no doubt that he was a crook.

With only minimal explanation Hunter convinced his friend in forensics to run the prints. Hunter had already run an FBI search under Owen Nigel Onan and had come up empty. In less than an hour forensics had a match. Onan's real name was Jacques Assad, and he had a rap sheet as long as one of Hank Aaron's home runs. There was no history of violent crime, but Assad had served time on three occasions for engaging in Ponsi schemes and other frauds. Unfortunately, there were no current warrants for his arrest. Graham hoped to change that.

Although the evidence was slim, Mather sanctioned the arrest of Onan on charges of fraud. Because all arrestees were finger printed, Onan would quickly realize that his true identity would be exposed. That knowledge alone would make him squirm and sweat. Even if an indictment was not forthcoming, Onan's days as Delphi University's VP of IT were numbered. Once Maria exposed Onan's past crimes in the *Scribe*, Sinduce and the Board of Curators would have no choice but to fire him.

Graham arrived home that evening with a large order of pasta con broccoli and salad from the Olive Garden. A light, refreshing Soave complemented the meal. Andean music (a gift from Maria) serenaded him as he contemplated the day's events. He loved the melancholy sound of the quena—perfect music for a chronic depressive like him. However, he also liked the joyful music of the Andes produced by the zampoña and the charango.

Ethics was clearly the theme of the day. Graham had such a visceral reaction to the news of all the dirty deals that Onan and his fellow thieves were up to that he had to restrain himself from stalking Onan and assaulting him in some dark ally. A strong sense of right and wrong had been the one enduring gift that Graham's Catholic upbringing had given him. As he matured, Graham was forced to admit that ethical decisions were not always black and white. He had to face questions like "does the end justify the means?" Making a choice about abortion, war, freeing a hostage all required that one might have to do something evil to accomplish good. At some level utilitarianism provided a partial answer to this dilemma; one should make the choice that provides the greatest benefit for the largest number of people. However, that assessment was often quite difficult to make. Joseph Fletcher's "situation ethics" offered another perspective. Good ethical decisions could not always be based on universal principles. Sometimes violation of an ethical principle was the more moral decision. For example, in some situations it might be better to lie about something than to hurt someone's feelings.

Philosophers also debated the origin of man's moral code. Kant had argued that man had an innate sense of moral obligation. Modern psychology, however, had totally debunked that myth; children were born hedonists with absolutely no moral conscience. The strength of the emotional connection that a child develops with his caregiver forms the basis for a sense of obligation to the caregiver. Hopefully, over time these positive feelings generalize to a natural empathy with all humans. Children who do not have this affirmative experience can become oblivious to the feelings of others, making it less likely that they will act according to the golden rule. Another topic that confronts both the philosopher and the criminal justice system is the issue of how free an individual is to make moral decisions. Both philosophers and criminologists have concluded that humans do have enough freedom to make ethical choices in most situations. However, both professions make provisions for reduced responsibility for crimes of passion and when a person is threatened with bodily harm. Also perpetrators with diminished intellectual or psychiatric capacity are held less culpable.

Graham had no doubt that Onan and the others had acted freely and were totally responsible for their actions. He had to find a way to prevent the great harm to the campus and the community that their ethical lapses would cause. Moral retraining for Onan and the others in prison was another goal of the philosopher detective.

CHAPTER 57:
MARIA FLORES NOVEMBER 13

Maria Flores was becoming as frustrated as Hunter over the Elly murder investigation. Both were convinced that Margo Elly knew her killer, because there was no sign of forced entry. Graham and O'Rourke had interviewed numerous suspects, but they still had insufficient evidence to indict any of them. As she took her morning walk along the Lethe River she carefully reviewed the case against each of the suspects, hoping that she did not forget any of the facts.

The autopsy report and crime scene evidence were puzzling. Margo Elly had not resisted being handcuffed by her executioner. The easiest way to explain this fact was to assume that she, not only knew her killer, but had previously had a romantic relationship with him/her. Mike Hammer, of course, was the one suspect who did have prior experience handcuffing the victim. Melissa Hope was a question mark. Had she replaced Mike Hammer in Elly's bed? Although her students would have been shocked to learn that their professor had a lover, Maria knew from her own experience that most people were ignorant of the love lives of their co-workers. Margo Elly was unlikely to have consented to being handcuffed by Primal Man, Savage, Spearman, or Onan. Of course if the killer had surprised the victim and displayed a weapon, she might have been shackled with no resistance. Under these circumstances she might have chosen to remain passive, buying more time to make an escape or be rescued. None of the suspects could be eliminated under this scenario.

Maria tried to imagine herself in the victim's place—handcuffed, staring up at someone who was taking great pleasure in repeatedly whacking her thighs and abdomen. Even if the blows were inflicted with minimal force, Maria could not conceive of herself not recoiling when the strikes were delivered. If your arms and wrist flinched in the manacles, wouldn't there be at least some minimal bruising?

Unable to draw any conclusions Maria collapsed onto one of the benches that stood outside the entrance to Hades. This section of the Olympic Forest was almost tropical in nature. The plant life was densely compacted in this woodland. One could see and feel the heat and humidity rise from the ground. Many species of birds created a constant cacophony of sound. Suddenly Maria was inspired. She had been reviewing the evidence from the perspective of the potential suspects and not from the viewpoint of the deceased. She had forgotten one of the main lessons of relativity theory. Truth is always somewhat subjective, dependent on the perspective of the observer. Nearly all of her questions had focused on the motives and opportunities of the suspects. She needed to identify more with the victim. Had something happened recently to Margo Elly that made her more vulnerable to death?

This new outlook caused Maria to review all of the evidence quite differently, particularly Elly's connection with each of the suspects. With the exception of a questionable email nothing indicated any contact between her and Primal Man. Margo Elly's relationship with her husband had not changed in over a year. Other than the dubious email there was no indication that Elly and Jacob Spearman had interacted in years. Melissa Hope and Elly had a special relationship in the past, but now Hope was threatening her mentor with a charge of academic misconduct. Onan had the most to gain financially from the professor's death, but there was no proof of any contact between them. Finally, Savage's entire professional career was at risk because of Margo Elly's actions. After mulling over her observations for another fifteen minutes, Maria was convinced that she knew who had killed Professor Elly, but could she persuade the Yanquee cop with the indigo eyes?

Although she knew it was not a rational act, Maria felt compelled to consult the Oracle. Hastily she made her way to the temple, failing to even enjoy the multiple aromas from the bakery that waffed across the Agora. She hugged the little pixie who wanted to be her "guide to the future" and flew into the temple. The priestess smiled at her repeat customer, dispensed with her usual speech, and motioned for Maria to enter the sanctuary. The sweet smell of lilacs flooded Maria's olfactory lobes as she waited for the Oracle to speak. The sage recognized the journalist and spoke warmly to her.

"What brings the Chilean goddess to my temple today?"

"Oh wise one, can you tell me who killed Margo Elly?

"My dear, death rarely has a single cause."

Maria smiled at her own craziness as she left the temple. She didn't need the Oracle; she knew who had killed Margo Elly. Now she had to convince her shy, stoic lover.

Full of self-confidence Maria walked briskly to her apartment. She needed to carefully plan her presentation for Graham. She decided to wear her black jeans and red knit jersey that showed off her figure. She knew that this ensemble was Graham's favorite. Although she trusted her analysis, why not purchase a little insurance? She also decided to fortify her arguments by fixing empanadas. No way would Graham challenge her theory after he had devoured her food! Ravel's Bolero kept her company as she finished preparing dinner. The theme was simple, but powerful. The crescendo reminded Maria of her own march to the truth.

After dinner Maria laid out her theory. She believed that Margo Elly was too strong to have been scared to death. Therefore, her death must have been caused by an externally administered dose of epinephrine. Unfortunately, all of the suspects and the victim had access to epinephrine. She then carefully reviewed all of the other evidence in the case. Finally, she discussed her observations about the relationship of each of the suspects to Margo Elly as well as the deceased's own behavior prior to her death. Graham was silent as he carefully listened to Maria's deductions. Then he smiled; Maria had convinced him. Hunter's relief and excitement in finally knowing the answer to this mystery overwhelmed him. He lifted Maria off the ground and nearly broke her ribs with his embrace. Tomorrow he would return to Elly's home to see if he could find the evidence to confirm Maria's theory about Margo Elly's death. For a few moments both Graham and Maria remained silent. Then, the journalist cracked a small smile. She was supposed to be the intuitive member of the team, but she had been much more analytical than Graham. The outwardly stoic and logical detective had missed several important clues, because his feelings and intuition had clouded his judgment. Maria felt no need to tease her lover about his emotional self. She loved him just the way he was. Instead, she kissed him on the forehead and led him to their bedroom to celebrate their victory and work off the calories of the evening meal.

CHAPTER 58:
GRAHAM HUNTER NOVEMBER 14

Mike Hammer had agreed to meet Hunter at 6 pm after he got off work. Graham knew this meeting would be difficult. To clear his mind he strolled through the Olympic Forest, past the open field known as Hades, until he reached the campus boundary. Beyond the fence lay the desolate area known as Tartarus. It was a deep canyon that had been carved out of the earth by Trojan Lead. The landscape was totally barren. No animals or plant life could be seen for miles. When it was windy, lead contaminated dust filled the air. Hunter thought that this was an appropriate destination for Savage, Spearman, and Onan. Slowly, he retraced his steps through the majesty of the forest and prepared himself for his encounter with Mr. Hammer.

Hunter could not help but notice how shaken Hammer was as he greeted him at the door. His voice cracked and sweat dripped from his body. Graham motioned for him to take a seat on one of the forest green sofas.

"Sir, your wife probably died from complications due to a massive dose of epinephrine. At this point we do not know if the epinephrine was produced naturally by your wife's body in reaction to an attack, or whether someone killed her by administering the drug externally. First I am going to ask you to retrieve the epipen that you kept on hand in case your wife suffered a bee sting. Then we are going to search your house for a syringe or an inhaler with traces of epinephrine."

After Hammer retrieved the epipen, he and Hunter began their search. The first stop was the first floor bathroom. Elly's epinephrine inhaler was not in the medicine cabinet. A search of Elly's bedroom, dining room, and the living room also failed to uncover the inhaler. Similarly, an exploration of the second floor rooms and S & M chamber produced nothing.

Their last stop was the kitchen, the scene of the crime. A built in trash compactor stood less than a foot from one of the barstools where Margo Elly had been found. The evidence technicians had found nothing suspicious during their investigation. Nevertheless, Graham examined the compactor; a milk carton and a cereal box were the only objects present. Hunter then opened an adjoining cabinet that contained pots and pans. He spied a double boiler at the back of the cabinet, removed the lid, and discovered an inhaler. He had no doubt that laboratory analyses would find traces of epinephrine.

Hunter suggested that the two men conclude their search and talk in the living room. Once again Hunter chose the seat that he believed Margo Elly occupied when reading her mysteries. He closed his eyes for a few minutes and meditated, but once again Margo Elly's spirit failed to speak to him. Lacking any new insight he turned toward the widower.

"Mr. Hammer, I know that you and your wife were having marital difficulties. Do you know if your wife was under any other type of stress?"

"Like I said, detective, Margo and I did not talk much."

"Did she ever talk to you about the Women in Science Fund or her patents with Smith Pharmaceutical?"

"No."

"Did she ever discuss any problems that she was having with her experiments?"

"No."

"Did she mention a Dr. Melissa Hope?"

"No. Detective, what is this all about?"

"Sir, I think that your wife committed suicide. Dr. Hope, one of your wife's former students, was going to accuse her of academic misconduct. I think that your wife was the person generating false evidence against all of the suspects, including you. She probably sent fake emails to incriminate several suspects. I am fairly certain that your wife was not raped; she staged the entire scene to throw suspicion of her death onto others. She even made you a target by leaving your souvenir bat next to her dead body. She probably used the bat to inflict the bruises on her thighs and buttocks, clearly reminding the police of the sadomasochism that the two of you had previously engaged in. However, we found no semen or other DNA evidence indicating that you (or anyone) had sex with her on the night of her death. Finally, your wife would have had just enough time to dispose of the inhaler and clasp the handcuffs around her wrists after she had breathed in the fatal dose of epinephrine."

"It's hard to believe that Margo committed suicide, especially after seeing her lying on the kitchen floor with all those cuts and bruises. She must have been awful desperate to disfigure herself."

"Actually, none of her injuries were very serious. Moreover, she could easily have ripped her own clothes and broken the wine bottle and glasses before she inhaled the epinephrine."

"My God! Poor, Margo! How hopeless and alone she must have felt."

"You are very forgiving, Mr. Hammer. Most people in your situation would describe her behavior as cruel and malicious."

"Perhaps, but they did not know Margo like I did. Behind her competent and haughty exterior was a little girl that was frightened of any type of failure."

"Mr. Hammer, we cannot prove that your wife killed herself. All of the other suspects, including you, also had access to epinephrine. Consequently, for the foreseeable future we can only classify her death as suspicious. Even if we determined that the inhaler did contain epinephrine, we cannot prove that she committed suicide unless her fingerprints are found on the inhaler. Your wife appears to have thought of everything in planning her death."

Once the interview was completed Graham remained in the living room for a few more minutes. His first thought was one of self-blame. He had made a tremendous blunder in his investigation by not spending more time addressing the motives and stresses of the deceased. He had not gone beyond the information that Judy Lacky had given him about Elly's state of mind. Had Maria not taken the time to understand the victim's situation, the case might never have been solved. He should have been more of a rationalist and looked for the real substance behind the sensory data (fake email, staged rape, file folder with articles by Savage and Spearman, etc.) that Margo Elly had manufactured for him.

After chastising himself for his mistakes Graham spent the next few moments trying to sense the desperation that Margo Elly experienced as her dreams crumbled about her. She must have felt very much under siege and very alone. Graham could not escape the conclusion that many people were responsible for Margo Elly's death. The moralist in him hoped that all of the suspects would pay some price for their hand in this tragedy. Before leaving he took one last look around the living room. Kate Chopin's novel *Awakening* was still on the end table. Graham smiled. He had missed the significance of that clue on his first visit. Now he understood Margo Elly's motivation. The poor woman felt trapped like Edna Pontellier and could no longer face life. Hunter then reacquainted himself with the other books in her library. She clearly loved mysteries. Elly had staged a fantastic "who done it" that would probably never be resolved by the official legal system. She had achieved her own distorted sense of justice by manipulating evidence such that her enemies had become the primary suspects in her death. Moreover, she had led the police down one blind ally after another. Yes, Margo Elly had played Hunter for a fool, but Graham had the last laugh. Unlike Margo Elly he was still very much alive. Maria Flores had resurrected him.

EPILOGUE

The Delphi Oracle continues to entertain and inform both the tourists and residents of Delphi, Missouri. She recently informed Kevin O'Rourke and Kathy O'Malley that they would have a long life together and many children. The Oracle also writes a gossip column for the local equivalent of the National Inquirer under the pseudonym of Cassandra.

Delphi University has once again become a tranquil four year liberal arts college where parents send their children to be educated and protected from the dangers of urban life. No signs of Primal Man, Darwin's Disciples, or the New Amazons can be found anywhere on campus. The new President, Father Dominic Alongi, has made great strides in creating a new campus culture that is more civil in tone without sacrificing a vigorous debate between competing ideas. A new program in Gender Studies has replaced the Program in Male Studies and the Women Studies Program. The Museum of Medicine will not be built, because the new Board of Curators for Delphi University withdrew its contract to sell the Olympic Forest to Trojan Lead. Thus, the Elysian Fields and Olympic Forest continue to provide inspiration and refuge for all the residents of Delphi.

The office of Innovative Technology (IT) has been eliminated. The former director, Jacques Assad (aka Owen Nigel Onan or ONO) is currently serving a five year sentence at the state penitentiary in Potosi, Missouri, for accepting bribes and misappropriation of government funds. Onan spends his time reading the works of L. Ron Hubbard, Ayn Rand, and Sun Lee Moon. His next reincarnation undoubtedly will be a religious experience that involves levitating money from some yet to be determined dupe.

The new Board of Curators unanimously accepted President Alongi's recommendation to terminate Professor George Savage for moral turpitude based on the report of the committee on professional conduct. Maria Flores had convinced several of Savage's victims to testify against him before the committee. Hilda German accepted President's Alongi's offer of a one year sabbatical to complete a book on the love lives of the Bronte sisters. Professor German has surrendered her military fatigues for long underwear, a parka, and snow-shoes as she tries to keep from freezing to death at the University of Manitoba.

Liz Gold, Donald Speak, and Bertha Sinduce took early retirement from the university. Gold's goal is to become the TV spokesperson for "Losing Weight with Chocolate." She is currently at a spa for the rich and obese, trying desperately to shed one hundred pounds. Speak spent thirty days in an alcohol rehabilitation facility drying out. Unfortunately, sobriety didn't suit him and he fell off the wagon within a month and retreated to his cabin in the Canadian wilderness. Speak takes some consolation in knowing that his inquiries helped expose Onan. Bertha Sinduce spent six months in a psychiatric facility suffering from catatonia. She is now a performance artist with an avant garde company that focuses on human movement. The artists include: "Human Pretzel," "The Blob," "Jade Stick," and "Mountain Peaks." Sinduce's stage name is "Stone Face." She is the last act in the show and her skill is to remain perfectly still without moving a single facial muscle until the last patron has left the theatre. Her longest performance to date is two hours.

Jacob Spearman remains a salesman for Jones Medical Supply. Sally Heater still works with him, but she has been promoted to administrative associate and receives 20% of Spearman's sales commissions. Their current sexual relationship is left to the reader's imagination. Mike Hammer now lives with his parents in Chicago and spends most of his time coaching youth soccer.

Maria Flores received a Pulitzer Prize for her series of stories on Delphi University, including the Passion with Protection scandal and the intrigues of Onan. She now works for the Bradenton (Florida) Examiner. She lives in a small bungalow on Anna Maria Island with her new husband, Graham Hunter. Hunter is currently taking philosophy classes at the University of South Florida while he ponders his next career. Every evening Maria and Graham take a long walk on the beach together. They enjoy watching children feed and chase hundreds of birds that gather on the beach at the close of the day. Often dolphins entertain them as they swim and feed near the coast. When their walk is ended they retreat to their favorite bench beneath a huge Australian pine to watch the sun descend into the Gulf of Mexico. Sunsets at Anna Maria are as variable as the motivations and feelings of those who gather on the beach to bid the sun farewell. Sometimes one cannot see the glow of the sun because it is hidden by dark clouds. Other times the sun is a bright orange ball that lights up the horizon. However, more often than not, thin clouds partially hide the sun, and its light is dispersed and reflected into a myriad of colors and shapes that keep changing as the sun slowly retreats from view. As the sun disappears the human witnesses are left with an experience that they cannot describe or understand completely, but one which brings them solace and causes them to humbly contemplate their place in the universe.

ACKNOWLEDGEMENTS

My wife, Maria Calsyn, read and edited many drafts of this manuscript. More importantly, she provided encouragement throughout the ten years that it took me to complete this project. Rebecca Pastor and an anonymous reviewer provided insightful and detailed critiques of earlier versions of the novel. Drs. D. P. Lyle and Eduardo Slatopolsky provided important medical and forensics consultation. Technical assistance regarding information technology, particularly email, was given by John Van Emden. Dr. Michael Griffin shared references regarding evolutionary psychology, sociobiology, and the effects of testosterone. Dr. Sally Ebest made many suggestions for the feminist index. Dr. Scott Decker advised the author regarding police investigation and the criminal justice system.

ABOUT THE AUTHOR

R. J. Calsyn is professor emeritus of psychology at the University of Missouri-St. Louis. He has published over one hundred articles on gerontology, social support, the working alliance, program evaluation research, and the problems of mentally ill persons who become homeless. He is married to Maria Calsyn who is his editor and partner in life. They split their time between St. Louis, Missouri, and Anna Maria Island, Florida.